KINGPIN'S NANNY

EVIE ROSE

Copyright © 2024 by Evie Rose

All rights reserved.

No part of this book may be reproduced in any form or by any electronic or mechanical means, including information storage and retrieval systems, without written permission from the author, except for the use of brief quotations in a book review.

This story is a work of fiction. Names, characters, places, and incidents are the product of the author's imagination or are used fictitiously. Any resemblance to actual events, locales, or persons, living or dead, is coincidental.

Cover: © 2024 by Chloe Maine. Images under licence from Deposit Photos.

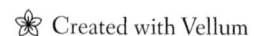

❦ Created with Vellum

1

BELLA

23RD DECEMBER

"Nanny Bella, do you think Santa will bring me everything on my list?"

I look up from where I'm wrapping my boss' present, and regard six-year-old Ivy. She worries her lip.

"Well, you have been very good." I'm lucky to be a nanny to such a lovely kid.

"I have!" she says in that earnest little voice. "I've really tried."

"Did you tell your Uncle Lucas what you wanted?" I can't even say my boss' name aloud without my heart racing. He might be a scary, tattooed mafia boss, and overly demanding, but between how he is with his orphaned niece and his sheer silver-fox gorgeousness I can't help my reaction to him.

Ivy's eyebrows pinch together. "I don't know if Uncle Lucas would like it."

"There are many things your Uncle Lucas doesn't like." Amongst them, his nanny attempting to flirt with him. "But if he can, I'm sure he'll tell Santa, and Santa can bring it for you?"

Ivy considers this with all the intent focus of a child. "Can I whisper it to you?"

Ope, this means I will be responsible for passing on this request to my boss.

"Of course," I lie. "Though it would be better—"

"I want a mommy and daddy," she blurts out.

"Oh Ivy." I stretch over the presents and gather her into my arms. I don't even say anything about the pronunciation of mummy. Mr Knight grumbles that the books I read to her, and the children's television we started to watch so she could know what was being discussed at school, is a bad influence, so I usually correct her when she uses an American word. But not now. This isn't the moment. "I'm so sorry."

She snuggles in and it hits me all over again how lucky I am. I'm an orphan too, but I landed on my feet. I have a great job, that's well paid. A little girl cares for me, it's Christmas, which is the best time of year.

I love a man who will never be mine. But I have a place in the world, and what more can a person ask for?

I shouldn't feel lonely.

"There's nothing Santa can do about that." I spent my whole childhood asking for the same thing. "But your uncle loves you."

"Sometimes he growls at me," she says, peering up from my lap.

"I know." Not as much as he growls at me. I sigh. "But he always comes to say goodnight, doesn't he?"

Every evening, I put Ivy to bed, and at exactly twenty to seven Mr Knight tells her one story and kisses her goodnight. He turns out her light at seven o'clock. No later. No sooner. He reads to her and does all the voices, but it's his own husky baritone that makes me swoon.

Honestly, everything about Lucas Knight makes my knees weak. He has permanent black stubble on his square jawline, like it grows out the moment he shaves. There are streaks of silver through his black hair, and it has a slight curl and falls over his forehead. I know most girls of my age wouldn't be thirsty over a man with white in his hair, but it works perfectly on my boss, matching his eyes. And oh my god, his grey eyes. He has the longest black lashes that make his eyes pop. I swear he could be in mascara adverts and make even more billions than he has as a ruthless and deadly kingpin. Add that to the fact he towers above me—I think he's at least six-foot-four—and has broad shoulders, yeah.

Definitely model material. Except for the tattoos, which are carefully concealed by the suits he always wears. But in the summer, we went to the beach for the weekend, and I saw his chest. I've basically never recovered. Beneath that neat facade, my boss hides muscles covered with black ink in swirling patterns, and a scatter of dark hair. He even has that V of muscle at his hips and the happy trail that points down to the place I had to look away from because I was blushing so hard.

I long to trace all those contours of his body. The hair, the muscles, the tattoos. And what makes it worse is that while I'm obsessed with how my boss looks, he never spares me a second glance.

In short, I don't know who is more excited—me or Ivy—about the twenty minutes precisely that Mr Knight allows for the task of his niece's bedtime.

Like a King's Cross train, he runs exactly to time. He'll sometimes have dinner with us too, and it's impossible persuading Ivy to eat her vegetables on those days because her uncle eats so few greens, I'm surprised he doesn't have scurvy.

I have stopped saying how much I love my veggies after I once said, "I love a big eggplant," and he just looked at me, no hint of a smile, and replied, "We call it aubergine in London".

No twinkle of amusement or shared look of acknowledgement of what that vegetable means in internet emoji. Nope. He really, really doesn't want to flirt with me. *Possibly* because my jokes suck. But really, don't powerful billionaires as attractive as him have a moral responsibility to give crumbs of hope to the pathetic, horny—if inexperienced—girls they turn into puddles of hormone every day?

Clearly not.

And aside from his diligent care of his niece, Mr Knight has a reputation for having very few morals. King's Cross—my boss' territory—somehow manages that anyone who has wronged them gets lost on a journey and never returns. It's one of the biggest transport hubs in London, and I think no one dares mess with Lucas Knight for fear they'll grind the whole city to a halt.

"He does tell me stories," Ivy acknowledges. "But I've never had a mommy and daddy, and all the girls at school do."

"Do they tease you?" I ask, perhaps a little sharply.

"No."

Thank god. I don't want to even imagine what Mr Knight would do if she was being bullied.

Ivy pouts as she thinks. "Do you think Uncle Lucas will let me call him Daddy if I give him a really nice Christmas gift?"

"Maybe." I'm not at all sure what would melt Mr Knight's heart if five years as being a de facto single dad hasn't. "The picture is really lovely."

"I think it needs to be better wrapped."

I blink. I've no idea where this has come from.

"What about the special wrapping paper we were working on?" It's really just colouring in, but I've drawn patterns on big sheets, and we've been filling them with bright crayons. It looks super cute.

"Yes!" Ivy smiles happily, and I return it, wishing I thought that the right Christmas present wrapping would bring me what I most want too.

Maybe I'll get a new dress on my afternoon off. If I'm draped somewhere seductively—or as close to that as an awkward virgin twenty-three-year-old gets—Lucas will take pity on me and give me what I want for Christmas too.

In fact, what I'm going to buy tomorrow is far naughtier: a sexy Santa costume.

"I'll go get the paper," I tell Ivy, and she springs off my lap as though she was never on the verge of tears.

For the next hour, I watch Ivy more than usual as we work together on the design-your-own wrapping paper. I drew a train pattern on this one, with holly, stars, and Christmas trees. Ivy and I agreed Lucas would like it.

My phone buzzes, and I jolt.

It's unexpected. I have everything set to silent—except Mr Knight's number in case he calls, but he never does—so I can keep all my attention on Ivy. But I do have one new app: OnlySantas.

Ivy is opposite me, happily colouring in stars. Surely it's okay, just this once?

I pull my phone from my pocket, and there on the lock screen is a notification that makes my heart race. The OnlySantas icon jaunty little present looks so innocent.

It's a lie. OnlySantas is an app for people who love to watch festive, sexy fun. Camgirls and guys dress up and while some just talk, many do *way more* than talk.

Late last night I checked with Mr Knight after he closed Ivy's door that what we agreed to when I began employment with him was still the case: I could have Christmas Eve and Christmas day off. He confirmed with all the charm of a bear woken early from hibernation and shown a rotten fish just out of reach. I've heard rumours of what happened to the previous King's Cross kingpin when Mr Knight took over. To only be snapped at and scowled at made me think I got off lightly.

I have been working for six months without a break now, which I'm pretty sure isn't legal, but mafia bosses make their own rules. It was a stupid impulse to sign up for OnlySantas, I know that. But after my attempts at flirting with Lucas have been as effective as flinging tinsel against a granite wall, I wanted to be seen. I want to feel desirable. I have two days off this year to do that. I'm going to make these days count, and also be properly festive.

And it worked. Someone has seen me on OnlySantas, even though I was too shy to post more than a promise of a show with the site's recommended everything for costs and stuff, and a picture of my white and red painted toenails.

I click the notification, then stare in shock. The exclusive rights to watch my whole performance on Christmas

Eve have been bought. And it's thousands. They've paid in advance, and their screen name is *YourBoss*.

My head swims.

Lucas.

I glance up, as though just thinking the word could summon him.

Has the man I've been hopelessly in love with since we met purchased my entire debut camgirl? That's insane. But how could he have known? It must be a coincidence. There are a lot of mafia bosses in London, and not all are famous.

But my heart has leapt to the conclusion that maybe he'll finally see me as more than just his employee, because that's what I most want. Being honest, I was going to fantasise that my boss was watching me while I took off my clothes for strangers anyway.

I check the start time of the show again, as though it might have changed without me looking. Seven o'clock. I have plenty of time to make myself nervous and crazy. But also—I'm leaving detailed instructions for Ivy's bedtime routine, already printed out ready. Mr Knight always finishes at seven. It could be him.

I close my phone and shove it back into my pocket. Picking up my red crayon—what could be more festive—I draw a smiley face on the paper, then colour it in, then look across at Ivy. She's still concentrating on that one star.

She doesn't know how my whole life has changed.

And while she's hoping the perfect gift will get her uncle to say he's her dad, I'm wishing for something far more difficult. She wants him to change his name, I want to change how he feels about me.

My boss has been a grump all year. And now it's Christmas, and while I won't see him in person, I'll be able to dream he's on the other side of the screen when I try to be sexy. Even if it is impossible, I can still wish that this Christmas he'll view me as more than an employee, and be *my* grump.

2

LUCAS

The previous evening

I fucking hate Christmas. As if it weren't bad enough that I lost my sister five years ago at this time of year, I have to give the love of my life permission to stay away from me. Apparently, it's unreasonable to expect a nanny to not have Christmas Eve and Christmas Day off.

The mouse I'm clicking around with on some shitty website that's full of useless ads and orange banners that mean nothing cracks as I clench my fist over it.

Fuck. Another thing to buy from this hellhole site.

I bash "computer mouse" into the keyboard so hard that when the search offers me a keyboard and mouse combination, I hesitate. Maybe I should get that. Bella is causing high levels of frustration, so more breakages are almost certain. I sort by price and buy the top result without looking.

Being a billionaire has some advantages, although not ones that allow me to have what I really want: my niece's nanny in my bed. That's filthy. Forbidden. Wrong.

If only it didn't feel so right. If only my cock didn't think she's the only exciting thing in the world. If only she weren't objectively the most beautiful woman in the world, and far too young for my shit.

I'm tempted to just buy the expensive thing for Ivy's present and get it done quickly, but instead I painstakingly check the reviews and ratings to find the best e-reader for a six-year-old child. As I try to figure out the contradictory comments, I wish passionately that Bella was sitting in my lap, arm around my shoulders, and telling me the right thing to get for the baby I brought up.

In the end, I get the highest priced one. A tablet, with a pretty pink cover. I note the advice that I need to set up some sort of internet monitoring, so my niece doesn't stumble into something age inappropriate. Like my whole bloody job.

The software automatically flags recent websites that will be banned for a child user, and I glance at the list. Yes, I do think arms dealers are better off not being accessible to Ivy. She's dangerous enough with crayons. Then a website URL stops me dead.

OnlySantas.

What the fuck in my worst nightmares is *that*? Why

has it been flagged? It sounds like an innocent, happy-clappy Christmas hell-hole from some dystopian mind-fuck. Nauseatingly cute.

I click the link, and my brows descend to below the floorboards. There's an age check.

Not so innocent then.

I put in my date of birth, and it's another reminder that I am twenty years older than the woman I should only want to protect, but actually want to own and fuck until she screams with pleasure and comes on my cock four times a night. The only way I prevent myself from doing that is ignoring when she's sweet and funny, and restricting myself most days to five minutes in her presence while accompanied by my niece. She's an excellent reminder of why I mustn't touch Bella.

The website shows profiles of popular content makers, and I scroll down. It's all wholesome and filthy. Santas doing all sorts of twisted things with fake snow, and snowmen. Men with white beards railing elf assistants. I have to admit, it's fun, even if I absolutely do not want Ivy seeing this. This would be just right for...

Oh shit. My chirpy, sunshiney nanny.

Has she been watching a Santa Daddy do depraved things to Mother Christmas? I rub my palm down my face. No. I can't dress up in a Santa costume. I can't.

Can I?

It's torturing myself, but I return to the website tracker and check which profiles she has been looking at.

But no. The OnlySantas URLs all end with things like "profile set up" and "upload photo.jpg". Then I see it. NannyBella.

That's *my girl*. She's mine. She cannot do this.

My heart in my throat, I click the link.

There's a picture of her from the side and leaning back, face slightly obscured, dark hair falling over her naked shoulders. It's the perfect combination of alluring and teasing.

No details about what she'll do, or videos. I scan down the page, then I'm caught. A lot of people have already signed up for the free part of her show.

The red I'm seeing isn't the cheerful seasonal colour of the website. It's absolute rage.

I skim past the paltry amounts to be able to message her, or make a request, or whatever, and smash the button saying, "Buy Exclusive Time", and *thank fuck*. For an amount of money that might seem a lot to most people I can have her whole evening. Just to myself.

I don't even think. I have my credit card details in there and I book it before anyone else can. It's only once I have confirmation that there will be no public show, and that I have the only link that she'll stream to that I can breathe again.

Sweeping my hair back, I stare. I just spent enough to buy a small house on a sex show that I cannot watch.

3

LUCAS

Six months earlier

"Boss."

"What?" I snap, then sigh. I look up at my head of security. Weston has a studiedly neutral expression on his face that tells me I'm being even more of an unreasonable bastard than usual. I am, perhaps, a little intolerant of failure these days.

I sigh and look across at my niece, who is at the other side of the table reading a picture book. My sister's daughter peeks up at me through her dark curls, and my heart twists.

"The nanny is here. For the interview."

"She's early." That triggers concern. I'm more cautious now than five years ago. There's nothing like letting your little sister make a bad marriage to someone you counted as a friend to make a man doubt his judgement, and even years later, I'm still over-protective of my niece.

But I cannot continue to work on a fucking laptop while supervising a six-year-old girl. Hence the advertisement for a nanny. A lot of applicants later, we still haven't found someone.

"Can you stay here for me, Ivy? I'll be back soon."

She smiles agreeably and I turn with a rock in my stomach. She deserves better than me. The uncle who failed her.

I get as far as the door before Weston pauses and side-eyes me.

"Boss..."

"What?"

He points at his hair. I go to flatten my own unruly greying hair, and my hand catches. Muttering a curse under my breath, I tug off the unicorn hair clip that Ivy put in earlier. It took us three videos, and two attempts on *my* hair, to get Ivy's hair right this morning. I shove it into my pocket and stride away.

We *really* need a nanny. My men cannot see me with unicorn hair clips.

"The new nanny is waiting in the hall," Weston says. "I'll bring her through."

"It's alright." That's how we've done it for every other applicant, but being caught wearing sparkly plastic makes me eager to dismiss him. "Get back to your job. I'll take her through myself."

Weston nods and leaves me for his office full of screens, and I head through to the front atrium of the house. It's a triple-height space with sunshine pouring in, and standing with her head bowed, looking tiny and touched by gold, is a slim young woman in a pale-blue cotton sundress.

My heart bounces. Actually bounces, like a rubber ball, an untrained puppy, or a mafia boss discovering an unknown emotion: attraction.

For forty years I've never looked at any woman with more than indifference. I haven't touched one for half a decade.

I want to touch this girl. I want to slide my fingers through her fine, long, straight brown hair, and greedily caress her pale skin. She looks soft, and suddenly, as though they're woken from sleep, all my hard muscular edges crave that silk wrapped over them.

I halt in the entrance to the atrium, in the shadows while she's in the light, and in a fair world, I'd have a few minutes to admire her and collect myself. But no, she senses my presence, or hears my abrupt stop, and turns towards me.

"Hi!" Her smile is brighter than the sun. I'm blinded. "I'm Bella Harlow."

I stare at her dumbly. As she smiles at me, it's obvious

she's young. No more than twenty, at a guess. Half my fucking age.

But fuck, Bella Knight has a nice ring about it. She fidgets her hands, and there's no wedding band there. Saves a man from an unfortunate detour to death.

Please let her be lost. Or a prank arranged by my men. The post girl, a Jehovah's witness, selling cosmetics door-to-door. Just please, please, please let her not be...

"I'm here about the nanny job."

I've never believed in a god, but it's clear now that if there is one, he's a sadistic bastard with a sense of humour worthy of the London Mafia Syndicate.

"Come." I spin and pace away with long strides. I don't check if she's following, but there's the tap of her little feet behind me. I take her through to my office and when I settle into my black leather chair, I push it from the desk so there is even more space between us.

I think if I ever touched her, I'd never be able to stop. That thought echoes uncomfortably in my head as Bella Harlow, my new obsession, stands before me, hands clasped neatly.

There's a beat of silence.

Professional distance. That's what I need. She's going to be my employee, I need to talk to her about work. So I do. A man who sounds like me in a very bad mood barks out details about Ivy and myself, and the role Bella will have as nanny.

She smiles and nods eagerly, responding with the energy of a golden retriever puppy.

"That's great," she says when I've finished explaining there's a full-time chef who makes nutritionally balanced meals and snacks. "And you? Are you around much?"

It's going to be hell to stay away. I fold my arms. "I run the King's Cross mafia, including the rail transport system out of London to the North."

"Oh. So you're busy." Am I imagining the flicker of disappointment as she says that?

"Yes. I won't have time to supervise you." I mustn't. There's a pause and then I can't help it. I have to know more about her.

"Tell me about yourself," I snarl.

"I've been a nanny since I was sixteen." She smiles wistfully, seemingly ignoring my foul mood. "I've looked after both girls and boys, and I'm fully qualified. I'm sorry I don't have a printed copy of my CV, but I guess the agency sent it over?"

No, not that. *Tell me what you like. What could I buy you that would make you smile at me not as your prospective employer, but as your lover. Do you drink coffee or tea in the morning? Tell me whether you feel anything when you look at me. Tell me if you think you could.*

"Why were you early?" I bite out, instead of asking her to crack open her pretty head and let me see how she works. I'd like to understand all the things that would give her pleasure, then provide them each day, on tap.

She swallows and fear slides over her face, there and gone in a moment.

"What was that about?"

"What?" She's bright and cheerful again.

"That expression." I saw it, I'm sure. And it wasn't me. This girl isn't afraid of me. She didn't respond like that when I said who I was, but the reason she was early scares her, and I'm going to find out what it is. I'm not ignoring a flicker of fear from a vulnerable woman this time.

"It was nothing!"

Something snaps inside me. I'm around the desk and towering over her in a second. "Don't lie to me. You were afraid."

She trembles, her eyes big as dinner plates.

And FUCK. She's *more* scared now.

I take a deliberate step backwards and try to control the memories. Anger and regret boil inside me. Those times that my sister, Natalia, told me that nothing was wrong. The moments when she didn't manage to hide her fear, just for a split second, and I saw it, but I didn't understand it was fear of Bradford. I thought it was just fear of mafia life, or a mother's concern for her child.

I didn't know that it was fear of her husband. I didn't realise, and she didn't tell me, and *I should have known*. I should have protected her.

The fact I killed that cowardly bastard afterwards has never been enough. I strung Bradford upside down from the rafters of one of the King's Cross train sheds and set him on fire. It was wire around his foot, so he didn't fall and die quickly. He suffered, and I watched every second until he was more bones than man.

His skeleton still hangs there as a reminder to all the King's Cross employees of what happens to people who harm those I love.

She blinks, and I remember that I'm a terrifying, grumpy kingpin. No lightness. No affection. I don't smile and I don't let anyone into my life. I do not care.

Except that right now, Ivy needs a nanny, and I care for my own.

"Why did you quit your last position?" I try again with a different tack.

"They didn't need me anymore, and I had to leave immediately. That's why I'm early," she says quietly. "I'm sorry I disturbed you. I didn't want to be late, and I didn't have anywhere to go."

"There are a lot of cafes in King's Cross," I point out.

"I haven't got much money." Her smile is brave.

"Did they pay you what you're owed?"

She hesitates, then shakes her head. "Not yet."

That meant they never would. "How immediately did you have to leave?"

"They uh, decided to send their youngest child—she's only seven—to boarding school." Her voice holds a tremor of distress. "They didn't want to upset her by telling her in advance, so they didn't tell me either." She pauses, and

I can see her turning the situation in her mind, finding the positive. "I had enough time to pack up my stuff quickly."

Despite everything I just said about not caring, I'm furious. She isn't saying it, but they threatened her. Turfed her out in some way that made her think she'd have been in danger if she had stayed for one more minute. "Their reference is on your CV?"

"Yes, but—"

"That's fine." It'll be adequate information for me to find and deal with them. They'll find out that travel comes with a *risk*. "You have the job. You start today, accommodation is provided, and I'll pay you in advance."

"Thank you!" Her lips fall open and her eyes shine as she looks up at me. I have a flash of a vision. That pink mouth taking my cock as I tell her how good she makes me feel. As I violate her sweetness.

I step backwards, and fold my arms again.

"Don't thank me," I growl.

This girl, my god. I do not take women into my bed. I never had any enthusiasm for those drawn by power or danger, even before I was a kingpin. It's always been me and my hand when I wanted to relieve some tension.

I shouldn't employ her. She's a temptation made perfectly for me. I can feel an emotion rising that I've never felt before. I'm obsessed. I'm compelled by her.

Love.

I've fallen in love at first sight, with a girl who is almost half my age.

Fuck.

Removing myself from the lure of her perfection is a physical effort as I return to my desk.

I rattle off the perks of being employed by King's Cross—minus the travel discounts—and add that she'll have the whole of the sixth floor as her own space. That will keep her far away from my bedroom, on the top floor, but in my house. As I've talked, I've found her application, which thankfully includes her bank details. I pay an excessively generous advance via bank transfer.

"Thank you, that's very thorough. I was just wondering though, should we discuss time off?" she asks tentatively.

I scowl. Days without her? Absolutely not. I'm going to sound unreasonable, but no. She's not leaving my sphere of influence. "You're a nanny."

"I do need some days not working." She presses her lips together.

"Which ones?" I growl.

"Sundays."

"Before Ivy goes to school on Monday? No."

She blinks. "Saturdays then."

"You think I have time to entertain my niece every week?" I reply, as though I haven't put literally everything on hold to look after Ivy since the last nanny left suddenly to care for her ill father. I need her to back down on this, so I go for broke. "Do you consider my job unimportant?"

"No." She looks down, chastened. "No, of course not."

I let the silence draw out.

"What about bank holidays?"

"Are you looking for a part-time position?" I ask, the words dripping with sarcasm. I'm being a bosshole, but I cannot have her not here. I *need* her close. "This is your monthly salary, Miss Harlow." I turn my computer screen for her and poke my finger at the transfer acknowledgement that funds have arrived in her account.

"Oh!" Shock ripples over her. "That's really generous. Thank you!"

Ha. I've won.

Her gratitude is evident, and I've bought the proximity of a woman I can't have and who will torture my every waking hour. *Well done, Lucas.*

"But I just—" She smiles prettily, but sounds desperate to be away from me. Already. Fuck.

"You can have Christmas Day," I snarl. That's half a year from now. I'll figure out some reason to keep her with me by then.

"Okay." She steels herself, her spine straightening and her shoulders going back as she thinks about her options. It's a *very* large salary, well worth giving up her free time for. And she doesn't have anywhere to go. "And Christmas Eve."

I grit my teeth but give a terse nod. I admire her courage, even if I don't like the result.

"Come and meet your new charge." Rising from my seat, I cross the room and open the door for her. Nervously, she goes through, and I indicate the entrance to the lounge. She gets there a second before me.

I gravitate towards Bella, like she's the opposite side of a magnet. We both reach for the handle at the same moment, and our hands touch.

I freeze. That momentary contact is a shock. Our gazes tangle and time slows down. I stare at this woman who is closer in age to my niece than she is to me, and I wonder what Bella Harlow would do if I propositioned her. She says she needs a new job immediately. What if I offered her marriage to me, and a credit card with Mrs Knight written on it and a limit larger than the national debt of most countries. Would she say yes, and let me feast on her pussy until she came on my face?

I withdraw my hand and flex it, attempting to get rid of the sensation of her skin. I cannot do this. However much I need her, my niece's nanny is not for me.

"Mr Knight."

"Lucas." My voice is hoarse, and fuck, I shouldn't have said that. "Ivy calls me Uncle Lucas."

"I might not call you uncle," she replies with a bright, teasing smile. After I was a complete prick to her, she's still sweet and warm.

I don't return it, keeping my features flat, with no hint of the turmoil inside me.

"Thank you for the trial period. I'll take really good care of Ivy, I promise."

"She needs to like you." That's the professional approach, right?

"The most important thing," Bella agrees cheerfully. "If she enjoys cheesy jokes and bedtime stories, I think we'll get along."

This girl is a ray of sunshine. Ivy will worship her, albeit differently from the way I do.

I make a vague grunt in reply.

As we enter the lounge where I left Ivy, I'm careful to keep my distance.

Ivy looks up. She's not colouring anymore, and instead is on the sofa with her toys.

"Uncle Lucas." Her grey eyes, just like my sister's and mine, slide between Bella and me, then stick on Bella, widening with interest.

No wonder. Bella is exactly the person a little girl wants as a mother figure. Beautiful. Long swishy hair. Clear skin and sparkling blue eyes.

"Hi!" Bella seems to know how to deal with this situation better than I do. "I'm Bella. I've heard so much about you, and I'm excited for us to meet. What are you playing?"

Ivy comes over all shy, ducking her head and peeking up at Bella.

"Unicorns," she manages to say.

"Would you mind if I played with you?" Bella asks, kneeling so she's on the floor next to the sofa, a bit below Ivy.

I have the perfect excuse to watch Bella for a while. I'm checking that she's a good fit for Ivy—as though that's in doubt.

Ivy passes Bella a plushie unicorn with white hair, and Bella smiles like this is the thing she wants most in the world.

Oh fuck there's a lump in my throat. Bella would be such a good mother. I can see her with a bump.

My child. I envisage a gaggle of children, Bella standing tucked to my side as we watch them play.

My phone buzzes and I sigh as I check who it is. Artem Moroz, the Mayfair kingpin. Damn. I have more important things to do than talk to him. Like obsess over my new employee.

Today, whatever is happening with the London Mafia Syndicate is an annoyance, even if I am privately amused that they're called the London Maths Club because the Canary Wharf kingpin couldn't own the fact he's a mafia boss, so had everyone pretend to his wife that we were geeks rather than murderers. Can't say I blame him, and I've won a couple of the maths competitions for who gets to kill some idiot who thought the stupid nickname of the Syndicate meant they weren't dangerous.

"Knight." I answer the phone. A sense of duty and order prevails.

There's a pause, then comes Artem's distinctive Russian accent. "Is that you, King's Cross?"

"Yes." Unlike many of the London mafia bosses, I like to pretend I'm not entirely characterised by my territory.

"Good, I need your help. I'm going into Sussex."

I raise my eyebrows. "Not interested in life anymore, huh? There are helplines for this, but it's not my expertise."

"Thank you," he says wryly. "I'm aware of the risks. But there has been a kidnapping, and I might have to go and get her back to keep the peace with a very angry Essex mafia who aren't keen on their princess being seized from an arranged wedding."

"Let me introduce you to a little concept I like to call geography." I watch Bella say something animatedly to Ivy, and my niece grins. "King's Cross deals with transport to the North. Sussex and Essex are to the East. They're managed by Liverpool Street."

"Thank you for the lesson. I was aware."

There's a brief silence, and I don't give a shit. I'm just staring at Bella's adorable little nose.

"Liverpool Street. She's a scary bitch," Artem says.

He's not wrong. Tiffany Abara works closely with the Essex cartel, and although she's part of London, she's hardly a big cuddly bear under a growly facade like the Paddington kingpin.

"I thought since you work together..." he adds ingratiatingly.

"You thought you could ask me to ensure you have safe passage."

"Da, thank you." Artem takes my irritated reply as acceptance. "I appreciate your help. My best vodka will be yours next time we meet."

"Fucker." The truth is I don't mind helping the London Maths Club. "Alright."

I hang up and then talk to Tiffany, as promised. Part of the role of King's Cross is to smooth journeys in ways not usually seen by anyone else. I didn't really appreciate that when I took over from Bradford five years ago. I was his second-in-command, but I had to learn quickly that there was more than trains and cargo shipments to the job. There are politics that I'm still far too grumpy to manage effectively, but I've grown into someone who is King's Cross now, for all I would rather be Lucas Knight.

By the time I'm done speaking to Tiffany and making a trade for her help, Bella and Ivy are both sitting on the floor with toy unicorns strewn around them, and giggling together like they're partners in crime. I think two of the unicorns are flying somewhere, but my cold dead heart refuses to acknowledge that this is cute.

I don't want to join them. I don't.

The call with my duty to the London Mafia Syndicate, and being King's Cross, was a reminder. This is who

I am now. I might have been human once, but now I'm a monster.

However much I desire Bella, she's forbidden. Not just because she's far too young and innocent for a man like me. Not even because I failed once to take care of someone I loved.

No. Because I'm already obsessed with her. I want her far more than is healthy, and I know how that ends.

This girl is my soulmate. I knew such connections existed—I've seen the love between some of the London Mafia bosses and their wives—but I assumed those were about as likely for me as a unicorn-drawn train carriage. Which makes this situation all the more painful.

I will protect Bella Harlow with my life, and from myself. Even if that means keeping a professional distance. Even if it means she can never be mine.

4

BELLA

Christmas Eve

I'm fizzing with excitement, waiting for the start of my first camshow, to an exclusive audience who has paid an obscene amount of money to buy out my whole evening. But it's not the show, or the fact that I'm going to reclaim my sexuality that has me thrilled. Nope, it's the screen name that has taken up all my attention since I saw it: YourBoss.

Could it really be Mr Knight? There's no picture to give me a hint, but that also means my imagination is running wild.

When I set it up, I accepted the OnlySantas suggested start time, which was seven o'clock. And he always has finished putting Ivy to bed by then, so…

Maybe? I hope bedtime is going well. I'm sure it is. I left lots of detailed instructions.

I've been preparing for an hour, fussing nervously over the cute and sexy Santa outfit I bought this morning, and getting my phone in just the right place in my room so it captures me at a flattering angle and in good light, but doesn't show anything that might be identifiable. I don't want my boss finding this and sacking me for compromising his house or something.

The anticipation builds in me, and when I log on a few minutes before the appointed time, I'm a tiny bit sad that my patron isn't waiting. But if it's Lucas, he's still doing his precisely timed evening routine, isn't he?

I watch the clock, and the seconds tick like trudging home in the rain on a dark winter afternoon.

It gets to seven, and I hold my breath.

He'll be here. YourBoss. He has to be. It has to be him. He paid an obscene amount of money for an exclusive show.

It's only one minute after seven. That's nothing.

Two minutes.

My chest is full of contradictory feelings. I'm still excited, and nervous, but something cold and dreaded is congealing in my stomach. They don't want me? YourBoss hasn't logged on, despite the eye-watering cost.

I can't hold this cute pose with the skirt and a little smile much longer. Another minute ticks past.

My arm begins to shake.

It's been five minutes, and I break my Santa girl character, allowing myself to pout. The status dot of YourBoss remains grey. He's not watching.

I wanted to feel desirable, to have eyes on me that admired me, and I'm stuck with nothing except the knowledge that YourBoss isn't who I dreamed it was, and whoever they are, they don't want to look at me.

My boss is always on time. He's precise. Yes, he's grumpy, but the very idea that he wouldn't put his niece to bed at exactly seven o'clock is ridiculous. I've seen him kiss her forehead at that exact time for six months. With anyone else, I could believe he was incompetent on his own, and that without me there to steer it, bedtime was late.

But not Mr Knight.

I have to accept facts. After twenty-five minutes, there's no question.

It's not Lucas. If it were, he'd have logged in at seven o'clock exactly, after closing the door to Ivy's bedroom.

But whoever it is has paid for my time, and doesn't intend to take me up on the offer to use it.

That I know of.

Never mind. I can still do what I intended this evening. I lean over my phone and poke through the settings of OnlySantas. Surely I can stop the exclusive booking and have a public show instead?

But when I find the cancel button, it's greyed out. The information pop-up politely informs me that since the payment has been confirmed, and the performance started, there is no way for either party to reverse the transaction now, and the sale is final. There's also some warning language about how going outside of OnlySantas is not allowed for my own protection, blah-blah-blah.

I sit back.

If I'm honest with myself, I didn't really want to perform for strangers. There is only one pair of steel grey eyes I want on me: those of a man with silver and black hair, black stubble, and swirling black tattoos I wish I could touch. But Santa was never going to bring me Lucas Knight for Christmas.

Without YourBoss' consent, I can't even turn off the camera. And his active status remains stubbornly grey. He's not online.

And suddenly, I've got the solution.

I get back onto my position on the bed, arrange my sexy Santa dress, which is red velvet with white fluffy trim and a black belt, smooth my Santa hat, and look straight into the camera.

"This is for you, boss."

Given my lack of experience, what he would look like as he watched is a bit hazy in my imagination, but I keep my gaze on the camera as though it were Lucas' grey eyes.

"I want you," I say softly. "I've wanted you since we first met." I trail my fingers over my velvet-covered breasts. "And I hope you want me too."

Slipping the straps off my shoulders one at a time, I

imagine that it's his rough hands doing that, grazing my skin.

I'm channelling every sexy thing I've ever seen. Ads, movies, late-night television, and that slutty girl at school. I should have asked her for tips. I watch myself in the camera preview for OnlySantas, and try to ignore that YourBoss' activity indicator remains stubbornly grey.

"Do you like what you see, boss?" I push the neckline down and add, "Would you like to see my legs?" I drag up the skirt of my dress with one hand.

"Or my bottom?"

I shuffle around on the mattress. I can almost hear his deep, dark, severe voice telling me that he can't see me properly.

"Should I take off my knickers?" I blush.

It feels indulgently naughty as I nudge the cotton down, exposing my bottom, and my pussy too. When the fabric is over my knees, I replace my hand so I'm on all fours again, and I breathe through the embarrassment.

"Am I okay? Is this right?" I'd never dare to ask Mr Knight this, but in my mind, he tells me, "Yes, that's perfect. Good girl."

"I'm delulu," I mutter, but I shiver with arousal. Closing my eyes, so I can't see that there's no one watching, let alone the man I want, I turn onto my back. The dress is rucked around my midriff, so I wriggle it over my head. On a whim, I press the hat onto my head again, then recline on the pillows, totally naked now.

In the dark behind my eyelids, I see Lucas above me. I can't remember the exact pattern of his tattoos from that day at the beach, and I wish so much I'd had the guts to somehow get a photograph so I could examine and memorise him.

I run my hands over my breasts and cup them, then pinch my nipples daringly. It's not his hands—mine aren't big enough—but it's nice as I skim lower. My knees fall open.

When I reach between my legs, I'm not surprised to find I'm wet. Soaked, in fact. Thinking about my boss always does that.

"I wish you were here. I wish it were your fingers. And then, I wish it were…" My god, where does the bravery to say this come from? "Your cock. I want you to be my first. And my only."

There's a little shock of pleasure as I brush my clit. I wriggle back into the bed covers and imagine Lucas Knight's severe gaze on me. He's so grumpy, but at heart he's kind. I've seen it time and time again with him. He could be cruel—it's expected even, after all, what's an uncle if not wicked, or a mafia boss if not mean—but he's not. He's dark and growly in his tone, but his behaviour is always considerate.

Apart from my lack of days off, of course. But that hasn't been such a hardship, to be honest. If it weren't for my sexual frustration boiling over, I'd happily never have a day away from him.

"Please. I'm so empty. I need this."

My hand is moving of its own accord now, circling over my clit.

I'm certain Lucas would have the experience and maturity to make it spectacular. "I want you to teach me to pleasure you, and make me come."

Saying the words aloud makes it more real, as though he's listening in. The ecstasy mounts and I give my clit more pressure.

5

LUCAS

I can't look away.

Instead of interrupting her immediately, I stare dumbly at Bella's young, hot body finally exposed to me fully. I have a surreptitious photo of her at the beach, but this? Not just nude, but touching herself and moaning.

I'm instantly hard.

She circles her clit faster, and writhes on the bed, looking every inch the sexy siren, luring me to my death.

Fuck. Bella is the most beautiful sight I've ever seen.

Christmas will be even more fucking awful from now onwards. Inappropriate erections are bad enough when I look at my child's nanny, never mind if I end up with the association with red and white costumes. That Santa hat is all she's wearing, and her smooth skin is all on display. As is her wet, pink pussy.

The desire to plunge my cock into that needy little

hole is stronger than the instinct to breathe. How can I live without seeing her like this again? My need for her is overwhelming.

My hand hovers over my keyboard. I have to stop watching.

Now.

6

BELLA

I lift my hips in a rocking motion that somehow makes me even hornier.

"I wish you were here, instead of my fingers. I bet you'd be... Oh..." Even the thought of Lucas' cock inside me sends a shock of pleasure to my core. I squeeze my eyes shut and pretend he's above me, sliver eyes flashing, that dark stubble rasping on my cheek. My lips tingle with my own breath, but I dream that it's his as he tells me I'm his good girl, and to come for him.

"I want you. I'm so empty without you." It's ridiculous, but I'm enjoying voicing all the pent-up desires of the last half year. "Please. I need you to take me."

I imagine him pushing into me and when I touch my fingers to the little hole where he'd do that, I can almost hear his growl of approval, and it breaks me.

My orgasm is a quick peak, harsh around the edges,

but I like it. I moan and writhe through it as though Lucas was listening and watching.

I put on a show, and I enjoyed it. I pant, and enjoy the tingling sensation.

Ding!

I don't notice the sound immediately, distracted as I am by my receding orgasm still rippling through me.

Then there's another. Ding!

And it cuts through.

A notification from my phone.

Sitting up, I lean forwards. It's only then I remove my hand from my pussy, and my hand shakes as I reach for the screen then stop. My fingers glisten. My fingertips are very slightly wrinkled.

Wincing, I close my legs and clean my hands with the nearest item of clothing—my Santa dress.

My heart smashes into my ribcage. It's probably nothing, it can't be. It's just...

The icon next to YourBoss is green. He's live.

My jaw drops open. How much did he see? When did he start watching?

And he's left two messages in quick succession.

YOURBOSS

Get dressed.

Now.

I stare uncomprehendingly, but my body knows. All

the arousal and confidence I had drains away like I'm a sieve.

Whoever he is, he doesn't want me.

I think I might cry.

> Put some clothes on.

I sigh, but do as my unseen patron says, slipping on my cotton knickers, and tugging an oversized T-shirt over my head.

"Is that it?" I ask miserably once I'm covered again. I feel very small and stupid.

> Goodbye.

"No!" I didn't realise how much I wanted this, but the thought of whoever it is on the other side of this little mistake leaving is unbearable. "Why did you book my show?"

The dots bounce as he types, and I watch the screen as though I can will his response into existence. As if I take my gaze from it, he won't answer.

But the bouncing stops, and no text appears.

"Why didn't you turn up at the beginning?" I ask.

No reply. Not even a little bouncing ball.

"I don't get it," I say, frustration rising. "Why pay all that money and not watch?"

> It was a mistake.

Oh. Oh my, that really hurts. I don't want to be a mistake. My whole life I've been unwanted.

But he did book me. It wasn't an accident. He logged into OnlySantas, made a profile, entered his credit card details, and ultimately, he's here now. So I summon a smile that I hope is sultry and knowing.

"It doesn't have to be." Looking right into the camera, I run my fingers through my hair and stretch upwards, like I've seen other camgirls do. It's cute and sexy. Probably.

"We haven't had our exclusive." I've dropped to a breathy whisper. "We still can. I'm yours to direct."

I move my hands to my breasts and squeeze them together, leaning forwards to give him a better look. It doesn't quite work in my T-shirt, but there are no more messages from my patron.

"Tell me what you want me to do, Boss." Maybe he likes being called that, since he made it his screen name.

> I've paid you. That's enough.

"No. It's not." The protest is out before I can stop it. I wanted something more from this evening.

> More money?

7

LUCAS

"It's not about the money," she says softly.

> What is it about?

"I want to feel sexy and desirable." She shrugs and smiles sadly, still my sunshine even when she's upset. "I wanted you to see me."

My heart does a somersault, but she doesn't mean me. She means YourBoss, and she clearly doesn't think I'm actually her boss given what she was saying when I finally logged on.

Probably I'm too old for her to imagine I'd have any interest in her, but my cock has never been harder.

I shouldn't have stopped her. I wish I'd walked down to her bedroom, unzipped my aching cock, held her down, and told her that she asked for this.

I should have defiled her in that cute Santa hat, my face an impassive grumpy mask, as ever.

Unfortunately, I seem to have some morals left, so instead I'm going to sit through saving her from herself and then jerk myself raw on my own as I wish things were different.

"That's why I set up this evening's show. I set this up because I felt—feel," she corrects herself, "about as attractive as a squashed fruit cake."

The times I've shut down her flirting crash over me, and I nearly write, "Sorry". Then I come to my senses.

> I love fruit cake.

She huffs with dismissive laughter.

I'm tempted to point out that half the Christmas cake she and Ivy made, I stole to eat in my office. Bella is very attractive to me. Even more so than fruit cake.

Part of me wished I had been here from the beginning of her show, but that just wasn't an option. Ivy got really upset that Bella wasn't there at bedtime. Bella had told her she wouldn't be, but through tired snivels, Ivy said she was worried Bella wouldn't have anyone to spend Christmas with. I didn't have the heart to explain that Bella had *asked* for the time off. I certainly wasn't going to tell her that as we spoke, Bella was probably preparing for her evening's fun.

I nearly called Bella, multiple times. Ivy just

wouldn't settle. On any other night I would kiss her and let her get to sleep on her own. But there was no way I could leave Ivy tearful and unhappy. I thought it was a bonus staying with Ivy kept me away from the temptation of Bella.

I told myself it didn't matter, because I wouldn't turn up for the livestream anyway, because that would be filthy and immoral. I would only log into OnlySantas to ensure Bella had left and got her money.

I never expected to open a video link to the girl I love and want in equal amounts perfectly framed on her bed, sprawled out with only a Santa hat on and her fingers on her sweet, pink pussy. On display for me, like a feast for a starving man.

But it *did matter*.

I've been thinking of this the wrong way around, protecting myself. I should have turned up, because Bella deserves to feel as gorgeous as she is.

I sweep my hand through my hair and curse.

> You are sexy.

And I am going to hell for this. But some truths cannot be denied.

She looks down like a kicked puppy. "The man I want doesn't think so."

> Then he's an idiot.

"Don't talk about him like that!"

My eyebrows hit the ceiling as jealousy poisons my gut.

> A protective little elf, aren't you?

"He's great. He's just..." She looks wistful. "He doesn't want me."

I'll kill whoever this man is. I'm going to find out who he is, and end him. Who could possibly look at Bella and not want her? Who could resist being the person she loved and defended?

Someone who doesn't deserve her, the back of my mind whispers. *Like* you.

Usually, I'm exactly wrong for Bella, but tonight, I'm anonymous. Right now, I'm not her much older boss who shouldn't want his niece's nanny, for fuck's sake. For this moment only, I'm the lucky bastard who can comfort her.

> I want you.

A pleased smile creeps across her face. "Really?"

> Yes.

"I'm alone for Christmas, and that kinda sucks."

She doesn't deserve to feel unloved. Not when she is so very loved by Ivy and me. My heart goes brittle. I did this. I shouldn't have agreed to her having any vacations, at all.

Or if I'd given her time off each week like she asked for originally, maybe she could have been willing to be with us for Christmas, as she belongs.

"Are you alone?" she asks, a little wary.

I laugh to myself. Sometimes she's naive. I'm watching her sex show on Christmas Eve. Of course I'm alone.

> Yes.

And I mean that in every sense of the word. I'm alone right now, and I will be tomorrow too. I'm alone in the world.

"Then why didn't you turn up for the livestream?" she asks.

Because I couldn't. However much I craved it.

"You must have wanted to watch." She looks at me intently, as though she could figure this out through the screen. "You knew you'd be alone, and wanted company?"

I'm hit in the chest again. She doesn't understand the depths of how I need *her*. The issue is the chasm between us. Not just this evening when I'm separated by a floor and so much understanding from the woman I love beyond anything, but also for all the time before I knew her, when I was aware there was something missing from my life and didn't know what. From the last six months that I wish could have been different, and worst of all, for the risk she's leading me towards that might mean I lose her forever.

> Yes, I suppose it was. I'm alone, and I purchased your livestream because I thought I'd be less alone watching you.

Plus, if anyone else saw her perfect body on a livestream I'd get no work done until February as I tracked them all down and arranged for their deaths. Which isn't very Christmasy, even by my standards.

"We could keep each other company?" she suggests, almost shyly. "I'd like it if you watched me."

My mouth goes dry as she slowly pulls her T-shirt over her head. She looks right into the camera, straight into my eyes, and smiles as she rubs her nipples to points.

"Are you..." She pauses and gives a breathy little sigh. Then bites her lip. "Are you hard?"

> Yes.

I can't lie to her now, it seems. I'm always hard for Bella. And Bella putting on a show for me? You couldn't keep my cock down with three train locomotives and a dozen carriages.

"I want to see." The sparkle is back in her eyes.

I hate that I'm going to spoil that as I begin to type a response. It's a no, of course it's a no.

"Please. Please, I really need to see that someone wants me. That I'm doing it right."

> What do you mean, doing it right?

"Well..." She squirms. "The man I want never responds. I try to flirt with him..."

Unbidden, the time in the kitchen when she playfully flicked a slice of strawberry at me repeats in my mind. She was so sweet and precious and sexy in her little summer dress. I wanted nothing more than to defile her in it. Grab her hips, turn her around, pull down her knickers and bend her over the countertop, then fuck her little tight cunt hard until I came right up against her womb and filled her up. I wanted to take her raw and breed her, and see how pretty she was swollen with my baby afterwards. That was what I imagined when I jerked myself harshly off after I walked away without a word.

If I'd said anything, I was certain she would have heard the gravel of desire in my throat.

"Thing is," she adds, twisting a lock of hair around her finger and licking her lips nervously. "I'm a virgin."

The blood stills in my veins.

A virgin. My perfect Bella is untouched.

"Until I met this man, I've never wanted to have sex.

And now I have all these *feelings*. I have all this..." She presses her thighs together. "And he doesn't want me."

I want her.

"I thought being a camgirl would help me get over him. Reclaim this for myself, and be a sexy woman rather than just a..." She shakes her head and sighs. "I guess he thinks of me as a little girl."

My poor Bella.

> I don't think of you as a little girl.

I'm far too aware that she's a fully grown woman. That's rather the problem.

"Then show me." She has a determined glint in her blue eyes.

A string tightens up my chest. I can't really do this, can I? But for her... To eradicate whichever arsehole has been making her unhappy, and to maybe get my forbidden longing for her out of my system.

I huff a cynical and slightly sad laugh to myself. That will never happen. But I could have this once. I could have a cherished memory of when she *saw me,* and we indulged in this madness together. Even if she isn't aware of who she's doing this with.

"Please. I want to see your response to me. I want to know I'm attractive, even if you're not..." Her expression goes flat, then she bites her lip speculatively. "What made you use that screen name?"

Oh. Shit.

Well, that was a fine idea when I was just going to chastise her for intending to show herself on camera, wasn't it? Now though…

I pick up my laptop and take it to my bed, sitting onto the covers and resting the computer near me. I angle the screen down and glance around. Need to be careful to block out anything she might see that would reveal her filthy older boss is obsessed with her.

Checking the video in the preview box, my heart drums, but no. All that's visible is my midsection and bit of the pillows. I'm wearing perfectly ordinary and deniable white shirt and dark suit trousers—shit, cufflinks. I rip them off and roll up my sleeves, careful to only go just below my elbow where my tattoos begin. Thank god for "keeping a neat persona for the money laundering businesses". I didn't realise it would also be good for a dirty interlude with an innocent young woman I want to ravish.

She would have seen my tattoos on my chest during the summer, but wouldn't have seen below the waist, which is all that will be revealed now. I doubt she noticed, even.

"Look, it's okay," she begins sadly, and I smash the share button. "Oh!"

Immediately, I click off the audio. There's no way I can watch her and make myself come without moaning, and I don't trust myself not to say her name.

I palm my rock-solid cock through my trousers, and she watches with wide eyes, staring into the camera.

"That's it, show me your face, fuck." She's so beautiful. Of course I want to see the explicit, sexy parts of her. But the opportunity to watch her face looking right at me —or seeming to—is far more arousing.

"I've never seen a man's..."

I smirk and flick my belt apart.

She draws in a breath as I pull down the zip, my cock punching upwards against the fabric, eager for her observation. Do I want to be the first man she's ever seen? Fuck yes. First and last.

"You're... Wow." She's even closer to the screen now. Like she can't get enough.

I release my cock, shoving down my boxer briefs and then giving myself a lazy stroke. A small section of my ink is visible, but not much, and I relax slightly.

She'll never know it's me.

"You got hard from watching me?" Bella asks, her tone one of awe.

Oh, she likes that power, does she? I grip harder, and a bead of pre-come leaks out the top.

Yes

One-handed typing is tricky when I'm half-crazy with lust and can't take my eyes off the screen where she's watching me, entranced.

Fuck it. I want more.

> Give me something to watch, little elf.

She laughs and snatches up her red and white hat. "I'm supposed to be sexy Santa! Or Miss Claus, I guess."

> You look like a naughty little elf to me. Who needs a lesson.

That smile is sweetly inviting as she bites her lip. "I wouldn't mind it if the real Santa did that. I have a bit of a thing for older men. Well," she amends quickly. "One in particular."

I will not allow my jealousy to ruin this. I keep up a steady rhythm over my length, but it's hardly needed. Although my brain is full of ideas of murdering anyone who touches my Bella, my body is responding as it always does to seeing her: with the intense need to breed her and make her mine.

> I'm twice your age

"Ooo. Really? Do you live in London?"

I ignore her question.

> You're mine for tonight, not his.

"I know." But there's heartache laced in her words.

> Show me your tits.

"Yes, Santa," she says teasingly, but does as I tell her, shifting back so I can see her more fully.

I groan as her naked skin is revealed. Those pert little tits, fuck, I'd like to kneel over her and streak them with my come. Own her. I've held my lust in check for six long months, and now every depraved thought is in my mind, my body straining for release.

> Cup them

That's all the typing I can manage.

Confusion flickers on her face for a second then she gets it, running her hands down her chest and sliding her fingers under the yielding flesh.

> Pinch

Her moan makes me even harder, as though that were possible, and I have to ease off not to blow my load too quickly. She turns me into a horny twenty-year-old again.

> Spread your legs

She takes a deep breath, as though despite being a sexy minx earlier, now I'm here watching her, she's unsure.

Coyly, she inches her knees apart, revealing her pink folds, shiny with how slick she is. My fist at my mouth and I'm biting my knuckle as my wrist bangs away at my cock faster. Did I say I would be happy just looking at her face? I was a fuckwit. I'd die to lick her.

"Do you like...?" she asks. "Is it...?"

> I love watching you.

I shouldn't reveal that, but her pleased smile is enough to justify the risk.

> So fucking hot.

Her shoulders go back a bit, as though that praise gives her the confidence she needs. I breathe through the overwhelming desire, and control myself enough to type more.

> Is all that cream for me, my naughty little elf?

"Yes. I love seeing how you want me. How hard you are."

I want to fuck her so badly I'm lightheaded with it. She's just downstairs, in my fucking house. She's here, on the screen, horny, and saying she likes my cock. So close, and yet so, so far.

> Touch yourself and imagine it's me.

The skim of her little hand down her body has me obsessed with watching now. As she reaches where she's wet, and cries out as her fingers brush her clit, I jolt too, as though we're connected through the screen. Like her pleasure enhances mine, and vice versa.

> Go on

She makes a soft mewling sound and begins to circle her clit with one finger.

> More

"Oh!"

> Show me your achy hole.

She blinks.

> Wider

Her chest flushes pink as she realises what I'm asking for, but my good girl opens for me, showing that pretty pussy.

> Harder

She obeys, her back arching, pushing her naked tits towards me. I love seeing her like this.

> Want to lick your sweet bud

I accidentally hit send before I finish the sentence. I'm not as eloquent as I'd like right now, but I'm torn between giving her instructions and stroking myself, both for my own pleasure and for her to watch.

She moans and I echo her, thrusting up into my hand.

Her gaze is fixed on the camera, and while I know she is looking at my cock, I let myself think she's looking back into my eyes. I let the pleasure rise as I stroke up and down the shaft, all the way over the tip.

Bella goes pink at the neck as she gets more and more worked up.

> Come for me

Her eyes go hazy, and her fingers speed up.

"I'd like to be doing that for you," I say aloud as she begins to shake. "So beautiful."

I take in every detail as she moans and shudders. The Santa hat slips from her head, and her hair falls around her shoulders in a dark shining flood.

She mouths a word as she climaxes, and maybe it was boss, or oh, or nothing at all. But as I stroke my cock one last time, I see it as Lucas, and pleasure explodes through me. I come and it's harsh and intense and almost painful in its intensity. Despite my palm over my crown, there's a mess of reams of white. I shift on the covers, not wanting to get the evidence of my sordid desires over my laptop where they'll taunt me forever with this memory when I'm trying to work. And attempting not to find my ward's nanny, push her against the nearest surface away from prying eyes, and slake my lust on her lush little body.

It takes me a minute to recover, my mind blank as I just enjoy this precious moment with Bella. And even when I reach to type a message to her, I'm not quite steady, knocking the laptop.

"Lucas."

Panic flares through me. I'm sure for a second that I turned on the audio or something. But no, that's not it.

Bella is staring intently at the screen, seeming to have come closer again, so all I can see is her pretty face.

"Lucas." She blinks her big blue eyes at me. "That's the name of the man I'm in love with. He's my boss."

My heart does a jumping thing. I wonder for a second if I'm having a heart attack. Maybe I'm dead. I'm definitely dreaming. But no, this can't be heaven. I've never done anything good enough to deserve this.

"You're *my boss*. It's your screen name, Lucas."

I should deny it, or say this can never happen again.

"I saw the photo. As you moved the camera, it showed for a split second before you turned it off."

My obsession has outed me.

My hands shake. The framed photograph on my bedside cabinet. Fuck. I look at that image every night with my cock in my hand, making myself come while thinking of that trip to France. I took a single, precious photo of her in that demure swimsuit, and have cherished it ever since.

I can't reply. I can't lose her, and if that makes me a coward, so be it. I need her in my life. Maybe I could apologise, and she'd stay. Or fine, I'll keep her here by force.

"I know it's you," she says quietly. "Even if you won't admit it."

Then another piece clicks into place, like a puzzle that swings open a door into the light. I couldn't take in what she said just now, but she has been talking about a man she loves.

She loves *me*? I'm the one who made her feel that I didn't desire her?

No.

Fuck, what was I thinking? That ends immediately. I smash the video button and turn on the sound, so she can hear my voice.

"Come here."

She gasps.

I have no restraint left. Enough teasing. No more avoiding the inevitable. I love her. I don't care that I'm twice her age, or that she's my innocent little employee. I'm going to claim my woman. She will be *mine*.

"Now."

8

BELLA

He has a photo of me beside his bed. I remember the moment captured so vividly, even though I didn't realise he'd taken a picture. I had just emerged from the sea, and was watching Ivy on her bodyboard, my back to Lucas on the beach. My hair was stuck to my head and my shoulders were pink from too much swimming in the sun.

About a month after I'd started working for him, we went to the South of France. The summer had extended into Autumn, and I don't know what made Lucas decide to go away, but Ivy asked longingly one evening, and told him that I'd never been to France. And he sprung it on us a few days later. A weekend on a yacht exploring secret coves and Lucas rolling his eyes when I wouldn't drink more than a sip of wine. Not with so much water around, and the smooth teak decks on the boat.

I was attracted to him before, my tummy fluttering

inappropriately on our first meeting. But there had been just the three of us on that beach, and I fell even more for my severe boss seeing him make sandcastles with Ivy. We'd spent hours at the beach, and I peeked at him from under my lashes, unable to believe a man like that was my boss.

I was full of a tumult of new feelings. I'd never wanted anyone before, but Mr Knight I'd responded to the second I saw him. The sight of his chest—wide, muscled, his pecs covered with a fine layer of dark hair and his whole torso a piece of art in black and gold—had just added more layers to my attraction. I wanted him.

That made the fact he was cold to me all the worse. I attempted to flirt with him. Awkwardly, of course. I brushed a non-existent bit of fluff from his shirt—as if fluff would dare to settle on Mr Knight—and said that being by the sea suited him. I even asked him to sit with me after Ivy had gone to sleep, and we talked late into the night.

I was convinced there was something between us, but when we returned to London it was back to the same thing: twenty minutes at bedtime, and cool civility.

And he has a photograph of me next to his *bed*. I don't understand.

I take the stairs slowly even though I want to rush. I can't quite bring myself to believe any of this.

He knew all the time while I was putting on a show. Lucas watched me touch myself, and said those deliciously filthy things to me. He stroked his cock and told me I made him hard.

He said he *loved* watching me.

"Bella."

I look up to find him on the stairs, coming to get me. He stops when he sees my face.

He's reclothed himself, though his forearms are still exposed, his tan skin in contrast to the white shirt. I'm an idiot. How did I not recognise him, just from his strong hands?

Because I was afraid. I was terrified it wasn't him. I couldn't raise my hopes that someone really wanted me, because there have been so many times in my life that no one did. No one cared.

"Bella." He runs down the remaining steps and catches me in his arms, pushing me against the wall, pressing his body right against mine and looks down at me. A lock of black, curly hair shot through with silver falls over his forehead.

He's hot and solid, his dark hair-covered forearms braced on either side of my head, the muscles flexing. I feel so safe.

We look at each other, both breathing fast. I'm suddenly very aware of my thin T-shirt and my nipples brushing against his chest.

"I've dreamed of this," I confess in a whisper.

"I have too, little elf." He pauses and when he speaks

again, his voice is tormented. "But there are some things you need to know."

"What?"

"I stayed away for your own good, Bella. I shouldn't—"

"You should!" He left me alone deliberately? "I want—"

"Shhh." He kisses me hard, and I don't think he realises it's my first kiss. Because it's short and his lips are soft and firm and passionate. But it does achieve his aim spectacularly, as I can't speak afterwards.

"You're so young. And you're my employee, and innocent." The sadness in his tone crushes the hope in my chest. "I'm the head of King's Cross. I'd tear you apart."

"I like that you're older," I manage to say around the rising fear that he won't let this happen. Did he not mean what he said, and I've misread everything? "I think it's kinda hot that you're my boss."

"You don't understand," he says, but he doesn't move, as though the tug of being close is as strong for him as it is for me.

"Then help me understand." Frustration seeps in. He says I'm young, but I'm not a child.

Lucas drags in a long breath, then sighs, his brows low. Then he looks right into my eyes, his gleaming dark and metallic.

"I'm so in love with you, it's an obsession. It's more

than you might want to cope with. I'm going to need to know exactly where you are, all the time. I'll want you by my side. You're beautiful outside, but my soul calls out to be entwined with yours. If I started, I don't know if I'd let you go. I'd need to be inside you, constantly. I want to have you close, every day, and fit us together in every possible way that feels good. And when our bodies are old, and can't do that anymore, when we have the satisfaction of seeing our children grow up, and have babies of their own, and the sun sets on our lives together. I'd welcome that too, as a way for my soul to be even nearer yours."

He's taking my breath away. This really is a bit intense, but I don't care. I feel the same way.

"How I feel about you isn't rational. I'm crazy about you, Bella." He reaches down, opening a gap for me to escape the cage of his arms.

I don't.

Slowly, he encircles my throat with his hand. "I'm dangerous, Bella. I'm the kingpin of King's Cross, and you should leave while you can."

Arching up, I push myself into him. "I'm not going anywhere."

"I can't trust myself with you," he mutters, apparently to himself, and he squeezes the smallest amount, just so his fingers press in and his thumb is on my windpipe.

I rest my hand over his. He must be able to feel the

pulse in my neck, and I can feel his—a solid thump-thump-thump—over his knuckles. "I trust you."

He shakes his head slowly. "I'm a bad man, and destined to be worse."

"I don't believe it." Not this man who kept his distance out of love, and cares for his niece in that gruff, tender way.

He sighs and his grip loosens, drifting down to the stretched opening of my T-shirt. He caresses my shoulder, and I reach for his side, trying to urge him closer.

"My sister was married to the previous King's Cross kingpin—Bradford—and he killed her."

"And you killed *him* in revenge, and took over his territory." I nod. This is not news. Even I know to do a bit of background on a mafia boss I'm working for.

He swallows. "What's not known by most people, is why he killed her."

The air in the stairwell is cool, and the glass above us, open to the stars, suddenly feels exposing.

"Bradford was obsessed." Lucas looks down, not meeting my gaze. "He wasn't willing to share Natalia with anyone. He was older than her—we were about the same age, and we were friends of a sort when I first started working for him—and he didn't want her to have children. He couldn't bear the idea of not having her all to himself."

My eyes widen. I've heard the stories that the

previous King's Cross kingpin was unhinged, but I'm not sure why Lucas is telling me this.

"And now history is repeating, Bella. A King's Cross kingpin is in obsessive love with a much younger, vulnerable, sweet girl. And you don't even have a brother to look after you."

It clicks.

"You think you'll harm me?" He grips my shoulder tight, right on the muscle and bone that can withstand it, hardly painful at all. Not like my neck, that couldn't take it. He doesn't realise how he cares and protects me. It's instinct.

"I've never felt like this before," he says. "I haven't *wanted* anyone, or anything. I didn't care about the power and money of this job, or anyone, but now I can't breathe without *you*. I can't risk that turning into the sort of love that Bradford had for Natalia. He loved her, but he hurt her. And in the end..." He trails off sadly.

"He didn't love her, Lucas."

He's silent, then shakes his head.

"What if I'm like him?" he whispers, agonised.

"You're not."

"I'm obsessed with you, I want to consume you."

"You wouldn't hurt me." I'm certain of that.

He meets my eyes, and there's something savage and untamed in them. "You don't know what I dream about, little elf."

"Bradford hated that your sister was pregnant, yes?"

Lucas nods slowly, expression grim.

"But you don't feel like that."

"Of course not." His impatient snap, so similar to the grumpy responses he's given me over the last six months, makes me smile. "You should have as many children as you want."

"As many as I want?"

He tips his head ruefully. "Then maybe two more, just for me."

Happiness bubbles up through my chest.

"He was jealous and controlling. And I..." He swallows. Then he brings one hand down and cups my jaw with tenderness that almost breaks my heart. "I do want to possess you. I'd die to keep you safe."

"You can be jealous, and possessive," I whisper. "And when you try to control me, I'll know it's for my security."

"Will it though?" His eyebrows pinch. "Or am I doomed to be the same as my predecessor? In which case, I should—"

"Kiss me, and I'll prove to you that you're not like him," I interrupt.

He groans as he lowers his mouth and the moment we touch is pure joy. Then this kiss is just as hard and demanding as our first. But it's longer, and so sweet and filthy. He slides his lips over mine, and nips at me. When I gasp, he takes advantage, and plunders my mouth with his tongue.

His hands come up and tangle in my hair, tightening

and holding my head still, and his body presses me against the wall, trapping me in the best way. The slight tug on my scalp, the desperation in the sounds he's making, and the little whimpers—they're from me, I realise—make this the hottest moment of my life.

I'm putty in his hands, helpless to do anything but accept this scorching kiss and try to pull him closer, exploring his narrow hips and warm, muscled back covered with smooth cotton.

And when he pants, releasing my lips for a second, I take my opportunity.

"Ouch!"

"What is it?" He has drawn away instantly. "See, I told you I'd hurt you."

His brows lower and he's all horrified concern. Because of course he is. This man might be a monster, but he's *my* monster.

"It's nothing." I give him a sassy smile. "You'd never let anything bad happen to me."

There's a long, taut silence. Then he breathes out, and his shoulders relax.

"Fuck."

"I'm right," I add.

"You," he says as he crowds me against the wall again, and reaches for my bottom. "Are a naughty little elf. And the next time I give you pain, you'll be moaning because it's so good."

I wriggle closer and allow myself a self-satisfied smirk. "All talk, Mr Knight."

"You are so fucking dirty," he growls, and when I gasp, his lips hit mine hard in a kiss with more unrestrained heat than I ever thought I'd get to feel. He sucks my lip into his mouth and the smallest hint of pain zings right to my clit.

"And do you know what happens to naughty girls?" His voice is gravelly as he nibbles at my cheek, then my neck.

"Do they get stuffed with—?"

His laughter cuts me off and it's so unexpected I draw back and stare.

He's beautiful when he laughs. I mean, he's gorgeous all the time, but he's mesmerising like this.

"You'd like that, huh? Don't worry. You will be stuffed, and spoiled, and treated. I'll give you anything you want for Christmas, and all the other days of the year." The light grin fades from his face to something darker, and hotter. "But tonight, I have other plans."

He gathers me into his arms, then his mouth finds mine again and I squeak as he lifts me up, and I cling to him and kiss him as he takes the stairs two at a time up to the floor he and Ivy sleep on.

He pushes the door open with his shoulder, and barges in. His eyes gleam wickedly in the half-light. "Tonight, you're mine."

9

LUCAS

I elbow the door closed behind us, careful not to slam it since Ivy is just down the hallway, and for the first time in forever, I breathe easily.

I have her. Bella is mine.

Tempting as it is to throw her on the bed and get inside her as quickly as possible in a bare, raw, animalistic claim, she's put me through hell this evening. My teasing little minx.

I slide her down my body, relishing her every softness against where I'm hard. Especially my erection, that digs into her tummy. Then I set her onto her feet and step backwards. I rake my gaze over her, not restraining my need.

"Tell me you're mine," I demand. "Say you meant it when you said you wanted me. Love me."

"All of it," she answers immediately.

"I don't deserve you." She's far, far too good for me. But I will seize every bit of sweetness I can. I will ravage her.

Motioning for her to remain still, I step to the bed, then sit on the edge, arms crossed.

"Take off your clothes, like you did when you thought I was a stranger." My voice is harsh. I know she was thinking of me, but she doesn't realise how close she came to getting men killed because they'd seen the body that was meant for me.

Her hands shake as she reaches for the hem of her T-shirt and slowly drags it up, obeying beautifully.

The second that it goes over her head is deliciously vulnerable. She's revealed, her body exposed, and she can't see my reaction. Bella knows this time that she's taking her clothes off only for me, and that I'm going to take her virginity.

It's so much trust.

Then the moment passes, and she tosses away the T-shirt and licks her lips nervously. I grapple with the instinct to reassure her. Instead, I palm my cock through my trousers as I drag my gaze over her.

I saw her naked on that screen, but here before me, she is perfection. Her tits are small but perky, her hips flare out, and her belly is slightly rounded. So fucking young and breedable, she's the most amazing thing I've ever seen.

"And your knickers."

She nods eagerly and slips the innocent scrap of white cotton down her legs, bending and giving me a magnificent view as her hair cascades forwards and then she reveals the V of her legs where I'm going to rut her. Fuck, I needed this. It's all I can do not to fall on her like an animal, but she has some penance to pay.

When she straightens, her brow furrows.

"I want to see you naked too," she whispers, a little uncertain.

"You have to earn that," I reply cooly.

Her eyes go wide. "How?"

"Come here."

She's mid step when I snap, "No."

She freezes.

"You were very bad," I growl. "You were willing to give some other man what I own. The sight of your pretty body, your attention when you orgasmed—"

"I was only ever thinking of you—" she protests, and I can see the honesty in her face. But that doesn't mean I'm going to let her off.

"Crawl to me."

10

BELLA

"What?" I can't do that. I can't humiliate myself, even if the idea makes heat spiral in my tummy, and lower.

"Crawl to me," he repeats, the words low but hard. Leaning on the edge of the bed, he's sprawled arrogantly. His rolled-up sleeves have bunched up, revealing the first lines of his tattoos. His dark trousers have an intimidating bulge in them. He's huge. A tremor of fear and excitement rocks me.

For a second, I resist. I glare back at Lucas, and his grey eyes are stoney. Then as though I'm his puppet, I fall to my knees.

I'm totally exposed, and he's almost entirely dressed, neat and controlled as always.

I lower my torso and touch my hands to the wooden floor. It's solid, grounding me after the evening's unexpected events. Surprises like: my boss wants me. And a shock that I don't mind what he asks. I'll do anything to be with him.

"That's it," he says, then he crooks one finger, beckoning me.

The first movement is jerky and unfamiliar. But I keep my head up, and watch Lucas as I move, small shift by painstaking shift, across the floor.

This is degrading. My cheeks flush with embarrassment. I hate crawling on my hands and knees towards the man I need more than anything, but somehow, I love it too. I want it over with, but I'm taking in every second. And between my legs, I'm getting even wetter. I'm slick and puffy with desire, and the discomfort of the floor on my knees and pinch at my wrists only makes me hotter.

My breasts—small as they are—swing a bit as I move. Lucas' gaze roams over my body, taking in my naked bottom and my back.

When I reach him, I pause, unsure what to do.

Lucas has no such qualms. He reaches one tattooed arm down and cups my jaw. "Good girl."

A sense of calm floods me. I've never felt so blissed out. It's warm and floaty, like that moment before you slip into sleep.

"That was beautiful."

I can't speak. It's all I can do to not collapse. But I do give in to the urge to press my cheek into his palm.

"Mm." He shifts his hand down so he's clasping my neck, as though his fingers are my collar, and a pulse of arousal shoots through me. I moan.

It doesn't hurt. It's crazily reassuring, having him hold me from such a position of power. He could squeeze, but I know he wouldn't let anything happen to me. So when he pulls upwards, I understand, and rise to wobbly feet.

"Such a good girl for me *now*, aren't you?"

Oh god, I really, really want to be his good girl. All I ever wanted was his attention and his love.

"But you deserve more punishment, don't you think? For your dirty camgirl Santa antics."

My mouth falls open.

"Here." He guides me forward, but where I half expect him to have me straddle him, he brings my head to his side and grabs my waist. In a second, I'm over his lap, held on my forearms and knees on the soft covers, my bottom resting on his muscled thighs. I gasp as my nipples brush the cotton and my hip touches the hard heat of his erection through his trousers.

"I'm going to spank every thought of showing yourself to another man—"

"I didn't!" I only ever wanted Lucas.

"—Out of you."

"You're going to hit me?" I ask in a small voice, craning my neck backwards to try to see his face.

"Yes, little elf. I'm going to give you what you deserve —pink buttocks that will remind you not to torture me like that again—then I'll give you what you need. My cock in your tight virgin pussy, filling you up, and swelling you with my baby."

I pant with crazy, inappropriate longing, and then shriek as his hand comes down on my bottom.

"That's it." Lucas soothes the place he smacked, and I catch my breath. Then his palm smacks again and I shudder. The pain is a deep thud that my body can't distinguish from pleasure. I wriggle on his lap, desperate for some pressure on my clit.

"You like that, don't you?" he croons.

I nod frantically, and a whimper emerges from my throat.

"Say it."

"Yes!" I gasp out, desperate for more.

"Yes, what?"

I search for the right word, but somehow what emerges is, "Yes, Daddy."

He laughs softly. "I was thinking you'd go for, Lucas, or boss, or sir. But yes. That'll do. I like being your Daddy. Good girl."

The sound of Lucas pleased with me shoots heat right into my core. For a second I think we're done. Then another smack takes me by surprise, and it's even better than his praise. I don't know why I love this so much. But the next time his hand hits my skin, it's light and stingy, and then he strikes my tingling bottom again, and again, faster, without stopping. I never realised this was what it would feel like.

It's a connection between us, this erotic punishment.

"That's it," he murmurs between smacks. "You're taking it so well. Will you be my good girl and not cry out when I split you open with my cock?"

"Yes, yes." I'm incoherent. My nipples are rubbing on the cotton sheets and every part of me is sensitised. "Please, Daddy."

He strokes a finger down the crack of my bottom, and I gasp as he brushes over my back entrance then further down between my legs. He laughs softly. "Not tonight, but yes, I'll own you everywhere."

Then his questing fingers reach where I need him, and I groan like a tortured creature as he slips one finger into my folds.

"So fucking wet, aren't you? Did you save all this for me?"

"Only for you," I pant out.

"Except you didn't." His voice goes hard, and the next second he's smacked me again. "Did you?" He slides his fingers further this time, caressing my clit with utter confidence. I'm so worked up, I almost arch off his lap, and he tsks me, pressing a hand down on the small of my back.

"Stay still for Daddy." There's so much affection in his tone, I relax.

I really, really needed this. I craved Lucas being my tender caregiver, and stern lover. I didn't know that after so many years of looking out for myself—and then kids too—how I wanted to give over control to someone else and trust them entirely.

"Yes, Daddy," I whisper.

"Such a good girl," he replies hoarsely. "You're my best girl."

"I'll take anything you give me." And it's the truth. He'll love and protect me. Somehow this spanking emphasised that. I belong to him now, and that means he'll look after everything, including correcting me if my behaviour isn't what he wants.

"Mmmm." He gives a contented purr from his chest and traces little circles on my thighs and bottom. "You're so pretty in pink. I love seeing my marks on your skin."

"Will you give me a tattoo, Daddy?" I want his ownership branded on me.

"No."

There's a bite of disappointment until he grasps my hair, pulls my head to the side, and sucks at my neck so hard the pain makes me gasp.

"I'll give you love bites and bruises and slaps to ensure you know you're mine every day." He licks the place on my neck that's throbbing now. "Nothing so crude and concealable as a tattoo. You'll have fresh marks that remind you that you belong to me. I want you to feel my love for you is strong every day. It isn't a one-time thing. It won't be something either of us forgets, because it'll always be new."

Ohh I love that even more, and the sting on my neck is delicious. He'll never let me doubt because I'll have fresh evidence, somewhere slightly different each time I look in the mirror.

"This bit is beautiful." He dips and runs his fingertip over my clit and it's fire.

I jerk as the pleasure surges into me from him. This isn't the same as when I touch myself. Nope, it's like he has found a hidden place that sets me aflame.

"I wanted you so much when you showed me your sweet little cunt." He continues to stroke me. "I was in a jealous rage about the man you said you loved."

"It was you, it was always you."

"I know." The smack takes me by surprise this time, coming as it does from his other hand and further up my bottom. "But you didn't realise it was me watching, did you?"

"I needed you." Pushing into his fingers, I unclench my fist from the covers and creep it back until I touch his hip, then slightly further, and his hard length is under my palm.

He hisses. "Bella."

"This, Lucas. Please." I'm desperate.

"That's your reward when you come for me. Got to

make your tight virgin pussy ready, then you'll get Daddy's cock." He's stroking me faster, and I'm so close. Just a tiny bit more. I squirm.

"I love seeing you come." I hear the crack before the pleasure-pain shoots into my bottom, and my orgasm sweeps out from my core. My legs go rigid and the world tilts on its axis.

Or rather, when the pulses have receded and there's just the glittering sensation all through me from coming, I open my eyes and realise Lucas has gathered me into his arms. The world has shifted, because I'm flat on my back, and he's over me, looking down with an expression so savagely proud it shakes me all over again.

"I love you so much," he rumbles, and strokes my cheek before dipping his head to kiss my lips. "I'm going to do that at least twice a day, every day for the rest of our lives. It'll keep me healthier than that fruit and vegetable bollocks."

A delighted grin stretches across my face. "I'll make you eat vegetables too, so it's a long life of giving me orgasms."

"For you," he breathes against my lips. "I'll do anything."

"Really?" I'm so happy I could burst. I guess I kinda just did.

"Even eat vegetables," he says dryly, lifting his head and raising one eyebrow.

"Take off your clothes, make me yours, and give me a baby for Christmas?"

His arrogant smile makes my heart patter. "I will do all that, and more. You're going to come on my cock. Then the next orgasm I give you after that, I want to be with my tongue."

Despite having just peaked, arousal bounces in me.

"Now." I grasp at his shoulders, then reach for his trousers. "Now. Please, Lucas."

He rears up, and rips his shirt over his head. His tattooed chest and upper arms are revealed, and I greedily take in the sight of his magnificence. He's even more beautiful than I remember from that day at the beach, and more powerful than when I interviewed for the role of nanny.

Him kneeling over me feels like I'm being conquered in the best way.

"I love your tattoos." His naked chest is a months' long memory, and I only got a peek of more black curling patterns that frame his cock on the live stream earlier. I can't wait to see him fully.

He strips off his trousers and underwear in one movement. I draw in a breath. In real life, right here, it's intimidatingly big. Veins run up his length. I thought men needed recuperation time, but Lucas is sporting a truncheon, and the black tattoos around it and over his hips only add to how intimidating it is.

"See how hard you make me." He takes his cock in his hand and gives it two slow pumps.

I gulp.

"This is all yours, little elf. You're going to take it."

"Yes." I reach for him, because the edge of fear only makes my desire sharper. "I love you." Scary tattoos, massive cock, and all. I want him so much.

He slides his knee between mine, and pushes them apart, and the dominance of that move shivers through me. He leans forward, covering me, and I moan as his chest touches mine. Something hot and silky pushes onto my thigh. His cock. I shift my hips, so it notches between my legs.

"Oh god, you feel so good. So wet."

"Please, Lucas."

The first push has resistance. Like my body doesn't understand how much I want this man inside me.

"I'm sorry." He sounds strained and brushes a kiss onto my lips. "This will hurt."

"Do it."

It must fit. We're meant to be, but I hiss as the blunt tip of him spears into me.

"Let me in," he says hoarsely.

I tilt my hips, and everything releases in a rush. I cry out as he slides deeper. It stings, but eases immediately, leaving only a feeling of contentment mixed with excitement that's intoxicating.

"That's it. You're being such a good girl for me."

It's just like he told me on the stairs. Being close to him is filling my soul as surely as he's filling my body. Being joined with him isn't easy, or without the best sort of hurt, but it's *right*.

"Tell me you'll take all this pain as I stuff you full of my cock, and ask for more," he demands.

"Please, give me more, Daddy. I love you."

"Good." He kisses me. "Then you'll forgive me for this."

11

LUCAS

I withdraw an inch then slide my cock into her bare pussy deeper, and she gasps. She's tight and hot, and made for me. Being in her is an intense, sweet pleasure I don't deserve. But I'm going to take it anyway.

Finally. I've wanted Bella for so long. Having her under me, being partway into her, is intensely right.

I run one hand over her hair, holding still inside her, stroking her hair like I'm comforting a scared creature. "I love you so much. Let me in more, little elf."

"You're so big..." She breathes deeply.

"It's okay." I lean down and kiss her lips, and that feels even better than her soaking wet cunt. "You'll love that soon enough, trust me. Here." I take her hand and bring it to her knee, placing her fingers there and encouraging her leg up and out. "Open wider for me."

"Oh!" She shifts and the new angle takes me deeper into her. "Mmm."

"And the other one," I tell her, but it's not necessary. She has already pulled up her other thigh so she's almost hogtied. I kiss her with sweeps of my lips on hers and withdraw, only to slide back in up to the hilt.

"You're heaven." I still again, letting her get used to my invasion. We breathe together, in sync, and my mind is clear for the first time in years. Or rather, it's full of love for Bella. "Us being connected like this is the privilege of my life."

"I can feel you so deep, Lucas. I didn't know you'd be so close. I'm never going to let you go." Her tentative little fingertips explore my shoulders. "I want you like this forever."

I chuckle. That's no hardship. "With you is where I'm meant to be. I'm never going to leave."

I'm finally getting to let my obsession with her be unleashed, and it's like my body knows I'm home. I look and touch, *wanting to take all of her in*. I play with her soft hair and kiss her lips softly as though the lust that's urging me to ram into her is happy to wait while she breaks open. There's only her and me, and the pleasure that's waiting to be called to the fore.

Experimentally, she lifts her hips, and I groan at the way the small movement makes her pussy flutter around my sensitive head.

"Give me more," she whispers. "It doesn't hurt now."

A raw sound of need escapes me as I do as she asks, withdrawing then easing back in.

"Yes, please." My needy girl mimics my movements with her own, but limited by the mattress and me above her, she can't get far.

"I like to hear you beg. You're so perfect." I grab her breast, as I've wanted to since she arrived in my life, and grin as she's the perfect handful. There isn't the right angle for me to suck on them, given our size difference—she's a tiny thing—but I pinch one nipple then the other and she gasps. "I can't wait to worship these sweet tits as they deserve."

"Please." And this time it's almost a sob. I'm powerless to deny either of us. "Daddy."

The first full thrust nearly undoes me. She's absolutely flooded, and there's just her tightness and heat clenched around my whole length. Another pump and she makes a wordless sound of pleasure that's almost a purr.

"Yes, yes, please," she begs me, wrapping her legs over my waist and pulling me into her with her little heels dug into my back.

"As you wish." I do it again, this time with a roll of my hips that I think she'll like and the satisfaction when she jolts and scratches at my shoulders, babbling about yes and god and please is even better than the pleasure gathering from the way we fit.

Then there's a rhythm, and we're working together.

Me pumping into her, and Bella writhing up to make each stroke faster and harder. I'm getting lost in her. I'm not sure where she ends, and I begin.

"I don't think I'll ever stop fucking you, constantly." I want it to be like this forever. Her and me.

She grabs the back of my head, and I feel her nod in agreement as she pulls me down for another kiss. This one is sloppy and open-mouthed and goes on and on, sweet and messy.

"I love you," she moans, her hands in my hair.

"I love you too." I love her more than I thought possible.

What's ridiculous is that I can't even see much of her since we're chest to chest, but I'm more turned on by her than ever. She feels so right.

Reaching down, I find her slick little bud and at the first touch, she tenses around my length.

"That's it, such a good girl for me."

I thrust wildly. I pound her into the mattress, far harder than I should with my virgin girl. But she doesn't let go of my hair. Nope, she holds me tighter, and sobs.

"Come," I grit out. "Tip me over and milk my cock. Take all my seed." My balls pull up and tingle with an impending orgasm.

This woman. Fuck, she's so amazing.

"I'm going to fill you up and breed you. Let me hear my name as you come for me."

She clenches around me and screams, "Lucas", just as

I told her to, her eyes open, those innocent, loving blue eyes looking up at me with trust and hazy with bliss.

One more hard thrust, then another, and I explode. I empty into her, shuddering, the intensity of this moment slamming into me. It's love and lust and I almost black out with how much I needed this. She completes me in a way I could never have believed.

I collapse onto my elbows, breathing heavily, cracked open.

"Lucas, my god," Bella murmurs.

"Me too, little elf, me too." I slide out of her reluctantly, pulling her on top of me as I do, and wetness gushes out of her over my belly.

"Oh!" She scrabbles, but I brace both arms tighter.

"Nope." Gently but firmly, I raise my leg, so it's wedged between hers, plugging her. Keeping my come inside her. "I'll fill you more later, don't worry, but I want you bred with my baby as soon as possible."

She giggles. "This is a dream. I had no idea this would ever happen. You were so cold, and now you're holding me and saying you want to get me pregnant. This is surreal."

"Bred," I correct her.

"Bred," she whispers back, blushing.

And that's when I really know this was inevitable.

"My heart has been yours since you turned in that sunbeam in the front hall, and smiled at me brighter than the midday light," I admit hoarsely. "I've loved you since we first met, and I wanted all your soft sweetness for myself. One smile and you held my heart in your hands."

"Why didn't you say anything? You kill people willy-nilly, but—"

I shake my head. "I couldn't. I was your employer."

"Well, I do have a very lucrative start of a camgirl career..." she says teasingly.

I growl. "You're not going on camera unless it's only for me."

"Deal." She snuggles into my chest. "Exclusive shows whenever you want."

My arms tighten around her. "I'll never let you go. I tried to fight my obsession, Bella. Every time you flirted with me it chipped off a part of my soul not to respond."

The relief to have her with me is so good it's unreal. Like she flicked a switch and suddenly my life is filled with light.

"We'll make up for lost time," she murmurs sleepily and her body softens. It only takes a few minutes, and her breathing goes deep and even.

It's longer for me. I stay awake thinking about how I'm going to explain the fact that I've claimed Ivy's nanny.

12

BELLA

CHRISTMAS DAY

I wake to searing pleasure and an arm over my hips, holding me down. Before I can comprehend what's happening, I'm coming, ecstasy shattering through me like a wave.

Lucas.

My boss.

Another pulse sweeps down my shaking legs at that knowledge. This is the man I've wanted since we met, and he's pressing kisses to the folds between my legs as I gain consciousness. I can only pant in glorious disbelief as he raises his head, then after leaving a kiss on my thigh, his stubble a rasp that sets off more little shocks of pleasure, he sits up.

"Good morning." Lucas looks downright wicked in the shadows, silhouetted in black and white. He takes one of my legs and strokes his fingertips all the way up with a purr of admiration. Then my bottom is on his lap, I'm open for him, and he shoves his massive cock right in.

The sudden intrusion is a momentary pain, despite how sopping wet my pussy is, then it's only bliss as he hammers into me. The angle is unbelievable, the helplessness and luxury of being on my back as he thrusts hard, taking what he needs, is beyond anything I've ever experienced. It's fast, or I'm still half in a dream state, because need tightens in me again immediately, and I'm lost to the sensation of him and me together.

"Give me another, little elf," he growls, and then his hand is between my legs this time, stroking me, and with the feel of cock inside me, I'm shoved from all sides into orgasm.

I barely see Lucas's fierce, tender expression through the dark and my own fog of pleasure, but his roar and unrestrained pounding tells me enough. For now. As things come back into focus, I swear I'm going to get my mouth on him and enjoy watching him fall apart while I watch.

Lucas presses a soft kiss to my ankle, then pulls me to him. I wrap my legs around his waist, wet heat dribbling down my inner thigh, and before I know it, we're in his shower.

He washes me like I'm his favourite doll, tsking when

I try to do anything myself, and lathering shower gel over my breasts more than strictly necessary to clean them. But he makes me feel dainty and cared for, and when he lathers shampoo in my hair, gently teasing out the tangles we put in last night, I melt. I only manage glancing touches of his magnificent naked body.

It's only when he's wrapped me up in a fluffy white towel that my brain wakes up.

"Ivy," I say, horrified.

"Don't worry." He smiles with a knowing look, and my tummy flutters. My god, I will never get used to how miraculous Lucus' smile is. "She knows what happens at Christmas. We've had a routine since she was old enough to be excited by Christmas, and it's early. I woke you because I had to have more before I shared you for the day."

He's right. It's only just seven and still dark outside when we creep downstairs. Ivy is sitting under the Christmas tree, examining a present. The Christmas tree lights are the only illumination, and she's so cute. Warmth washes over me as I look at her. I don't know what tomorrow will bring, but I am sure this will be the best Christmas of my life.

"You didn't peek at any of those without us, did you?" Lucas rumbles behind me.

Ivy looks up, bright and happy and innocent. "I was just looking."

"Good." Lucas leans in and touches me lightly on the

cheek as he gives me a cup of coffee. His grey eyes gleam, and I can hardly believe it, but he's smiling. Like this is his natural state, and all his grumpiness was a dream.

I take a sip of coffee, and it's frothy milk and sweet with honey. Exactly as I like it.

"Now, shall we do presents?" He turns on a table light that glows a golden light in the living room. One hand catching mine and lacing our fingers, he sits onto the nearest sofa to the tree, and keeps our hands on his thigh, casually linked.

"Can I play Santa and give them out?" Ivy asks eagerly, bouncing on her heels.

Heat flushes into my cheeks. Playing Santa. Mm. Yes. Better that someone else does that, I think.

"You can be Santa," Lucas replies with absolute calm, then glances across at me, a teasing gleam in his eyes. "Bella will be my little elf."

We watch her indulgently from the sofa, our hands still interlocked, and the feeling that he won't let me go is even more magic than the perfect Christmas vibes of the pine-scented tree, warmth and snuggly glow of the lights on inside and darkness beyond the closed curtains.

Ivy has noticed something is different, and keeps casting curious looks over her shoulder, as she chooses the first present, which is her largest one, of course. It's gorgeously wrapped, and after obediently reading the card—from "Uncle Lucas"—Ivy rips off the paper with all the patience of a ravenous little tiger.

She gasps then squeals with delight when she finds it's the stables for her toy unicorns that she's been talking about since the summer, and opens it out fully, examining each piece. She might be the niece of a billionaire, but she's not spoiled. Ivy appreciates everything she's given.

Lucas and she clearly have a strict Christmas tradition, and it's that presents are opened one at a time, each person in turn, and savoured. And wonderful though her first gift is, it can't distract her from the others under the tree. After the initial thrill, Ivy scrambles back to her feet and selects another package.

Ivy gives Lucas the box I wrapped only a few days ago, shooting me lots of excited looks as she does so.

I watch his long, elegant fingers remove the ribbon, stroking it as he pulls it out. A frisson goes through me as I remember how he touched me last night. He was gentle and rough and if I sent Ivy to bed and put myself in ribbons I wonder if Lucas would undo me too?

"Billionaires are difficult to buy for," I mutter.

Lucas stops his unwrapping, tips my chin with one finger and looks into my eyes, pinning me with his eyes that seem silver rather than steel now. "It's a good thing that nannies are easy to buy for, then. We balance each other out."

Warmth skitters over my skin.

Then he focuses back on his present, sliding out the picture frame, and I hold my breath.

He takes it in for a second, then traces the abstract

design I painted on the edge with his thumb. It's a picture I drew in black pen, at Ivy's direction, and she coloured it in. It's a knight in full armour, but instead of a horse, he has a train. And then there's a little girl in a green dress—Ivy loves to lean into her name—and a woman. Me.

"Do you like it?" Ivy asks, her unicorns forgotten for now.

"I love it." Lucas looks up.

She beams at him. "See, there's you, and me, and Bella."

"Is this me?" He points at the picture of a little girl, a teasing smirk playing at the corner of his mouth.

"No, silly!" Ivy exclaims, and he laughs and pulls her onto his knee for a kiss. She hugs him back and for half a second I'm left out before Lucas hooks my shoulder and drags me in too.

"Thank you, both." The sincerity in his words makes my heart feel six sizes too big for my chest.

"Now Bella's gift!" Ivy is almost as impatient to give me my present as she is to open the rest of hers. "I'm going to get her the one from me!" She wriggles off Lucas' lap and the moment is done, but it was still so sweet I could have a sugar high for days from it. Probably will.

"Uh-uh." Lucas stops her in her tracks. "There's one in white paper under the tree that's for Bella. She's having that first."

"But—"

"No."

It's unbelievable how hot I find it when Lucas is stern.

The present is duly brought to me, and I thank Ivy as I take it. It's wrapped in thick, expensive-looking paper with a snowflake pattern, and tied with a silver satin ribbon. I turn it over carefully in my hands. I can't see a label.

"This is from me," Lucas says.

"Just you?" I ask, a bit confused.

"Yes. I bought it a few weeks ago."

I suppose I shouldn't be surprised by that given his declarations last night, but I still am. He's still my grumpy boss, after all.

Under the paper, it's a large, flat jewellery box covered in fine white velvet. Even though Lucas is a serious-minded billionaire, I half expect it to be a joke as I open it, and that there will be two sticky pieces of popcorn and a plastic spoon, but there isn't.

Instead, I gasp. There's the most stunning necklace I've ever seen. Clear stones and platinum twinkle in the cosy Christmas lighting.

I stutter things about how amazing it is, and how grateful I am, and he shouldn't have. Lucas brushes all that off and picks it up from the box. Sweeping my hair away from my neck, he lays the necklace on me and does the clasp, caressing my throat as he does.

It must look a bit much with my sweater and jeans, but I feel like a princess when I turn back and see the admiration in his eyes, and it sends a thrill down my spine. The way his gaze lingers on my chest says he wants to take me back to bed.

"Flawless diamonds for my flawless little elf," he murmurs.

"I'm not—"

"You are."

Obviously, I'm not flawless, but I don't argue more because I'm lucky. So, so lucky. He slings his arm over my shoulders as though this is the way we sit together all the time, and the necklace is a slight weight on my front that almost has symmetry. It's a security I didn't realise I wanted, wearing something Lucas gave me.

He leans in again. "It looks beautiful on you. But your real present is the baby."

"What did you say?" Ivy demands, looking between us suspiciously.

"Just checking that Bella liked her gift," Lucas replies easily as I blush Christmas-red.

There are more rounds of presents and whenever I lean forward too far, Lucas tucks me closer to him. Which is hardly a difficulty to cope with, so I lay my head on his shoulder. I receive a rainbow unicorn of my own from Ivy. I promise to play with her later. Then there are more gifts for Ivy than either of us, of course, including a tablet that Lucas has put a reading app on, and my heart fills at how good he is with her.

I've always liked Christmas for the sparkling lights in

the depths of winter, and the ideal of family harmony. But I've never felt like I was part of that joy until now. The morning sunlight is peeking through the curtains by the time there's wrapping paper scattered across the carpet, toys everywhere, and Lucas is on his second cup of black coffee.

Ivy has sobered as we've reached the end of the stack under the tree, and Lucas watches her, brows low.

"Don't you like your presents?" Lucas asks.

"I do! I really do!" Ivy says quickly. "It's just... Nothing."

And that's when I remember what she said, seemingly a lifetime ago, before I discovered Lucas had bought my evening as a camgirl. Ivy told me she wanted a father for Christmas.

My heart squeezes, because I had that feeling myself, every Christmas during my childhood. Every Christmas until this one, if I'm honest.

Ivy goes back to playing with the new unicorn toys, and I lean over to whisper into Lucas' ear. "She said she wanted a dad."

13

LUCAS

"Ohhhh." I look at my little niece and the weight of guilt is immediate. Like with Bella, I kept Ivy out because I thought that was best. I thought I was unfit. It's only now I can see that I hurt us both unnecessarily. "I'm sorry you two. I've been a terrible gift giver." But I'm going to make up for it.

"You haven't," Bella protests.

"But you'll need to help me." I have a plan, and it can't wait until I have the correct items bought. "Ivy, could I borrow two of those friendship bracelets you got for Christmas, please."

She got a whole box of them from a friend from her school and has already put some on the unicorns.

My niece tilts her head thoughtfully. "What colours?"

Amusement flares in my chest. Why did I think this was the easy way? "Gold would be ideal, but—"

"I don't like gold," Ivy declares. "I prefer green."

"Understandable," I reply with the seriousness this topic deserves. "Perhaps you could give me a gold one and a green one?" Blue is my favourite colour since a certain blue-eyed woman came into our lives, but I'll allow green in this case.

Ivy narrows her eyes, clearly reluctant to part with a green bracelet, but sorts through them until she finds two she feels she can spare. With solemn gravity, Ivy hands them over. I rise from the sofa and take them from her, pocketing the green one.

The friendship bracelets are designed for a child's wrist, and tiny, made with plastic beads and not exactly the classy and outrageously expensive jewellery I'd prefer to do this with.

Never mind. I take a deep breath and lower myself to one knee before Bella.

14

BELLA

For a second, I can't understand why he's kneeling on the floor. Then he's taken my hand in his and there's no air in the room as I hear his question as though I'm in a bubble.

"Will you do me the great honour of being my wife?" He slides the friendship bracelet over my finger, wrapping it around twice, so it's like a bulky double ring.

"Oh my god." I stare at him.

"You're going to get married!" Ivy claps her hands and bounces. "Can I be a bridesmaid?"

"She hasn't agreed to marry me yet," Lucas says with a twist of humour. "But yes. You can."

"Yes." I grab him by the shoulders and pull him up for a kiss.

"I'll get you a proper ring tomorrow," he murmurs against my lips then kisses me deeply.

"Oooohhh. Muw, muw, muw." Ivy makes exaggerated kissing noises.

For a second I think it's my laughter shaking him, but I realise when we part that Lucas is grinning too.

My heart is so full of happiness, I could float away.

"You kissed Nanny Bella."

"I did," Lucas says unrepentantly as he moves back onto the sofa. He makes a space between us for Ivy, who hops up into it and looks at us with suspicion.

"Now, I asked you for another bracelet, didn't I?" He pulls the other bracelet from his pocket.

"That's a *green* one," Ivy says with significant emphasis. "Green is my favourite colour."

Lucas nods and holds the bracelet out.

"I was wondering if you would wear a bracelet on your wrist to show that I adopted you, rather than being your guardian? Bella will be a Knight when we're married. Would you like to be Ivy Knight, and have our surname too?"

Ivy blinks, clearly not seeing the relevance of this.

"I'd like you to officially be my daughter," Lucas says seriously.

Understanding dawns and absolute joy brightens her face. "Can I call you Daddy?"

"If you'd like to, I'd be proud to be your daddy too."

Ivy squeals and throws herself at Lucas, who grabs her easily in a hug, and she babbles incomprehensibly. The sweetness of it is almost too good, and when Lucas catches my eye, I lean forward and am pulled into the hug.

The three of us are a family. It's more than I ever dreamed of.

"What did you mean that you'd be my daddy *too?*" Ivy looks up eventually. "Who else's daddy are you?"

I shake my head ruefully. Lucas should know better than to drop that sort of comment and think she won't notice. She's a smart kid.

Lucas glances over at me, a naughty gleam in his eye, and before I can stop him, says, "Just that there's someone else, very special, who will call me Daddy..."

"Lucas!" I whisper desperately. I do not want to explain my newly found kink to anyone, least of all a child.

"...when they're born. Because Bella and I are going to have a baby."

"A baby!" Ivy spins and stares at me in shock. "Is it a boy or a girl?"

Behind Ivy's back, Lucas winks at me.

"I'll always protect you," he mouths silently.

I sag with relief. I knew that. Of course I knew that.

"Will they be my sister? Or brother?" Ivy demands. "I don't mind which it is, so long as I can be their big sister."

"You will definitely be their big sister," Lucas replies calmly. "And we don't know yet whether it will be a boy or a girl."

It's on the tip of my tongue to point out that we don't even know if I'm pregnant, but one look at Lucas and I know his answer to that. If I'm not yet pregnant, he'll take great satisfaction in ensuring I am very soon.

And despite the improbability, I think I am.

"In a few months we'll be able to find out," I risk saying.

"If Uncle Lucas is going to be my daddy, and you're going to get married to him..." She trails off.

"Yes." The answer is obviously yes.

"Can I call you Mommy?" she says after a second, not understanding I've already agreed.

Lucas rumbles mock disapproval.

"You can call me *Mummy*. Or Mom, if you prefer." I squeeze her and she giggles. "We won't tell Dad that we use American words sometimes."

"I heard that," he grumbles, but his eyes are sparkling.

"This Christmas is nearly perfect," she says with a serious expression just like her uncle—or her now-dad.

"It seems pretty perfect to me." I can't imagine anything better. I have everything I've ever wanted. A family, security, love. The sexiest and most caring man in the world has asked me to marry him and have his children, and we have Ivy as a daughter.

"What would make it perfect?" Lucas asks indulgently.

Ivy gives us both the most angelic smile imaginable. "Can I have a puppy?"

EPILOGUE
LUCAS

23RD DECEMBER, 10 YEARS LATER

"Fucking thing!" I hurl the sticky tape across the room just as there's a knock at the door, and Bella slips into my office. She takes in my furious expression and the tape rolling to a stop on the floor, and her mouth twitches.

"Did it betray you, King's Cross, the London Mafia Syndicate, and good taste, and deserve to die?" she asks, deadpan.

Bella is wearing a slinky red dress with a subtle pattern that matches the lining of my suit jacket, and my heart pulses as I see it. She's mine, and I'm hers, and I love the little signs of ownership we have that are outwardly visible. Her wedding ring and engagement ring included, but the ones that take a moment of coordination are even more special. They speak of our continued bond.

But even seeing Bella cannot salvage me from this bad mood.

"No," I snap. "Worse."

She raises her eyebrows.

"I can't find the end," I admit, dragging my hand through my hair. There's a lot more silver in it now. Mainly caused by sticky tape. That and eight children, plus London mafia nonsense that puts the UN Peace Corps to shame.

My wife giggles and picks up the roll of tape. "Shall I help?"

I sigh. "I should have got the shop to wrap it. But oh no, I had to order it online like an absolute idiot."

Hips swinging, she crosses the room to my desk, and perches on the edge, just in front of my chair and begins to run her nail over the sticky tape, focused on the task.

Since Bella is here, the kids will be with "Aunty" Cath, our amazing nanny who is like a grandmother to them. She's sixty years old next year, and devoted. The family we were always meant to have. And both of us trust her, so when we need it, there are moments away from the kids, even when we ought to be leaving for an event.

"Mmmm." I run my hand up her leg. "I'm thinking I should unwrap *my* present rather than wrap up someone else's."

She leans into my touch, and gives a breathy little gasp.

"We..." She swallows as I squeeze her thigh. "Really shouldn't. We don't have time before the Maths Club Christmas party." She reaches for the scissors, and even as I draw a purring moan from her, sliding my hand over her arse, she snips neat sections of sticky tape, tagging each one onto the side of the desk.

"We shouldn't," I agree, and pull her to me. She squeals as I get her in my lap and kiss her. She tastes like mulled wine, and I groan.

"We always have enough time for you..." I reach under her silk dress and slip my fingers up the outside of her thigh and into her knickers. I stroke over the soft skin just in from her hip, and I can feel the slight raise of her tattoo there.

My name. And I know without looking that there's a love bite on her right inner thigh from last night.

In turn, I have new tattoos too. Our children's names down my lower leg, and Bella's name on my hip in the matching location to mine on her. And while I don't get bruises from my wife half as often as she does from me, I treasure them when I do.

"Are you wet for me, little elf?" I shift my hand across from her tattoo and cup her sex, then groan when slick heat drips onto my fingers. "You are. Did you bring me this juicy cunt to enjoy? Such a naughty girl."

"You make me like this," she whispers as she leans

onto my chest and our lips meet. It's a slow, sensual kiss at first, but within seconds it's open-mouthed, and my fingers have slid through her folds to rub over that perfect clit that was waiting for me. With my free hand, I grab her hair and wrap my fist in the silky strands, pulling her head back to break the kiss and reveal her neck.

I love to watch her from every angle as I make her come. Face-to-face is a favourite, but all of her is delicious, and as I feel for the exact place and set up the rhythm that I know makes her crazy I relish every detail of her expression. The little signs of arousal, like her pink cheeks, and the soft sounds she makes as I drive her higher.

"Lucas." Her gold wedding ring glints as her hands shake on my lapels. "Please."

"That's it." I increase the pressure, knowing she can take it. "I'd love to bend you over this desk right now."

"Now. Please." Her begging in that breathy tone breaks my resolve instantly.

I groan and have her off my lap and bent over my desk in a moment. Then I free my erection and plunge into her. No questions, no hesitation. Just parting her soaked, puffy pussy lips and shoving all the way home. She chokes and arches her back, and I grab her hips. The pleasure is so immediate and intense I almost black out.

The first thrust is heaven. The second is even better. Then I'm ramming into her like an engine piston, and I can't get out words, or let go long enough to tell her to touch her clit.

Thankfully Bella knows that though I prefer to be the one stroking her patiently to orgasm myself, when we need to be quick, I'm happy for her to help. Through lust-fogged eyes, I see her reach between her legs, and I feel her pussy tighten around my cock as she strokes her clit, her hand obscured from my sight but the movement of her forearm frantic.

I can't get out any words. I just pound into her, using my wife's perfect body in the way we've done hundreds of times before, just like this, and many more in other variations. But there's something special about these quick, furtive fucks that only serve to relieve our need for each other in the fastest way possible when we know it's hopeless. I'll want her again, far too soon.

I always do. I love her too much to not be joined to her whenever I can.

The familiar tension builds at the base of my spine, and my balls pull up.

Her cry as she comes is only a second before she clamps around my length. I ram home harder as she pulses, then my orgasm slams into me as hard as I've been fucking her. It surges up from my balls and through my cock. I shoot my hot come deep inside her, right against her cervix. And fuck, but after ten years and eight children, you'd think I wouldn't care about breeding Bella, but you'd be wrong.

I can't speak or more than grunt my ecstasy, but I fucking love filling her up. She'll smell like sex for the rest of the day, and when we look at each other there will be that secret between us.

I might be getting her pregnant right at this moment.

Her pussy drags more and more out of me.

We're both breathing hard as I withdraw and straighten my clothing. Bella doesn't move, collapsed as she is on my desk. I pull up the scrap of white cotton over her hips and flip down her skirt. Then I grab her by the throat and pull her upright, jerking her flush against my chest.

"I needed that." I kiss the top of her head and squeeze her to me.

"Not as much as I did." She turns and looks up at me, pure mischief on her face.

"You are the most distracting little elf." There was me thinking I'd instigated that. Ha. I'm putty in my wife's hands. "I love you."

"I love you too." She closes her eyes.

"But you are a very naughty girl." I lower my voice to a rasp. "And you'll pay for being a tease, and making us late. You're going to soak through your knickers and leak my come down your leg all through the party, aren't you?"

Her eyes fly open. "I should clean—"

"Don't you fucking dare," I growl into her ear.

She shudders with delight, and I run a possessive hand down her front, lingering over her breasts.

We breathe in unison, and I smile at the red and white of her outfit. Not quite like Santa, but a nod in that direction.

Then she looks back at my desk, and tilts her head. Picking up the Secret Santa present I was wrapping, she furrows her brow in confusion. "Lucas, you're sure *this* is for Secret Santa?"

"Quite certain."

With a snort of laughter, she puts it down. "Who is it for?"

"You'll find out at the London Maths Club Christmas lunch."

"Spoilsport," she says happily, and cranes back to kiss the side of my neck. Pure happiness washes over me. Bella and I had a Spring wedding almost ten years ago, with Ivy as a bridesmaid, and Bella looking breathtaking in white silk. Since then, it's been a blur of babies, birthdays, and perfect Christmases. I can never believe my luck.

My wife and kids make everything good.

"Mafia Christmas party, then I'm going to take you to bed properly later, and make you scream for that stunt you just pulled," I promise Bella. "Now wrap the present like a good girl, and be quick. If we're late I'll tell everyone it's because I had to discipline my naughty little elf."

"You're far too protective to do that," she giggles as she reaches for the wrapping paper and covers the gift in five seconds flat, with an efficiency that stuns me anew every time I see her do it.

"True," I admit. "You're *mine* and I don't share. Not even subtle details."

I take her hand and interlock our fingers, and we leave my office like that. Together. Always.

A few minutes later, the whole family is in the front hallway where I first saw Bella. The winter sun isn't as strong as the summer when it highlighted her like the angel she is, but it touches all twelve of us now.

Bella, Aunty Cath, and I are ushering everyone out the door when Sylvie's plaintive cry comes from near my knee.

"Daddy!"

I juggle eighteen-month-old Willma in my arms to look down at her.

Sylvie looks up at me, eyes shimmering with tears. "I haven't got my bunny ears!"

Oh fuck. A crisis of the bunny ears headband. They are critical to Sylvie's emotional stability, and we cannot go without them.

"Where are they?" We have a lot of organisation with so many of us, but apparently that cannot overcome the chaos of one of my middle daughters.

"The playroom." Her lip wobbles.

Danger, danger. I really should have been helping get

the kids ready to go out rather than allowing myself to be distracted by the excruciating Christmas tradition of Secret Santa, and my wife luring me into fucking her.

"I'll get them for you." I know how important these things are, even as I glance at Wilma, who will inevitably cry if I put her down. I head towards the stairs, which will be quicker than the elevator for just two flights.

"It's alright, Dad," Ivy says, ruffling Sylvie's hair. "I'm on it."

"Thanks." The gratitude comes from bone-deep. Or at least cartilage deep. My first daughter has a special place in my heart.

"No worries," Ivy says and whistles for her dog—she managed to persuade us to give her a puppy by the third Christmas of asking—and they take off upstairs in a cloud of glitter. Ivy has tinsel in her hair and wrapped around her waist, and her dog has tinsel on his collar. I suspect they'll match the outfits of her friends, the other children of the London mafias. I really shouldn't have agreed that the dog could go to a London Maths Club event, but Ivy assured me her pup would be better behaved than most of the Bratva boss' sons. That had the ring of truth, to be honest.

Willma gurgles, and I jig her in my arms a bit. Seconds later, the all-important bunny ears are on Sylvie's head, and we pile into the car. A scratch of regret gets through my skin that I have to spend time with anyone who isn't my family.

"Fucking Christmas," I grumble under my breath. Christmas is good for filthy sex with my wife, and nothing more. I refuse to believe otherwise.

"Dad!" Ivy laughs and elbows me, then cuddles her dog closer on her lap. "You love Christmas!"

"Hmmm." She's far too perceptive for a sixteen-year-old.

"You smile for all of December. Don't pretend!"

"Lies." I rub my face to hide my grin.

I suppose Christmas isn't so bad.

EXTENDED EPILOGUE
LUCAS

10 YEARS LATER – THE LONDON MATHS CLUB CHRISTMAS PARTY

"Honestly, I'm impressed," Bella says to me as she rejoins me at the adults table after checking on the kids. "The only red is the holly berries and poinsettias. No blood at all."

"Ivy hasn't tried to murder any of her brothers again?" I pull Bella down to me and kiss her head. Even after this many years, and in a crowded room, she still smells like heaven.

"Nope! Christmas spirit is in the air, and peace and goodwill to all annoying brothers, it seems. Sylvie still has her bunny ears on. She's sitting next to the Vasiliev's eldest boy and he's taking care of her."

I run one finger down Bella's bare arm, and she

shivers then smiles up at me as she picks up her fork to finish her dessert. There was a rather amazing choice this year of chocolate and orange spiced tart, sweet and tangy mince pies full of fruit and brandy, and classic Christmas cake with a thick layer of marzipan. The jugs of fresh cream and bowls of brandy butter have all been polished off.

I chose Christmas cake, of course. I always choose fruit cake if Bella offers it to me. My favourite.

The Christmas lunch has become a significant part of the London Maths Club social calendar, along with the Blackwood's youth art auction, and other charity events. And while I tease Bella about wanting all her attention on our mafia for our special time of year, I feel a glow of pride every year when I see how amazing the space we use for the Christmas party looks. There are at least a dozen Christmas trees—real ones that scent the room with pine—decorated this year with delicate shimmering baubles hung on red ribbons and little fake glowing golden candles. The lower branches had carefully wrapped chocolates that have mostly been raided by the kids now. I don't know what most of the decorations that cover the walls and the tables are really. They're pretty though, and they are arranged perfectly.

The biggest Christmas tree has a pile of presents underneath it, including the one Bella wrapped.

We've reached the point in the dinner where everyone has loosen their ties or smudged their makeup.

Suit jackets are over the back of chairs, and Mayfair is arguing happily with Richmond about the best types of bullets. There's festive goodwill all over the place, possibly correlated with the empty wine bottles.

"It's like a bloody zoo at the kids' table," Lambeth says, collapsing back into his seat. He's been gone for a while to check on his children, though not for the whole meal, and his bow tie is slung loose around his neck.

"Is that blood on your eyebrow, Lambeth?" Canary Wharf asks from the other end of the table. "I thought we said nothing sharper than a spoon after last time."

"That was an accident," Kane Anderson, the kingpin of Croydon says quickly. "And she has apologised and promised not to bring a knife again."

"I checked, no knives," Anderson's wife, Lily, adds.

"It's alright." Fulham shrugs. "I told him that chicks dig scars and tattoos."

Lambeth's wife, Jessa, reaches over and wipes the red substance from her husband's face, sniffing it suspiciously before sucking her fingertip. Lambeth groans and she winks in response.

"Cranberry jelly," she announces cheerfully. "I love my husband's jelly."

"Get a room," Duncan Blackstone grumbles in his broad Scottish accent, but he's smiling.

Lambeth grins unrepentantly and sweeps his wife's blonde hair from her neck to press a quick kiss there.

"How many kids do we have between us?" asks Lina,

Artem Moroz's wife. "Bella, you must have a head count?"

"You honestly don't want to know." Bella takes a swig of wine. "Suffice to say we're outnumbered. If they try to overthrow us, we're toast."

"Your lot, King's Cross," Lambeth says with more gravity than a man should when he's just had fruit based products wiped from his face, "are like a pack of hyenas."

"Thanks." I grin. "Hyenas are amazing hunters. The lions usually scavenge off hyenas, you know."

Lambeth looks askance at me. "It's not theft if it was yours by rights."

"There is plenty of food," Bella interjects. "No need for scavenging." She shares a look with Lambeth's wife, Jessa, and they both laugh.

"Did you know alpha female hyenas have a girl dick?" Bella adds, innocently.

I choke on my own breath.

"Kinky." Jessa's eyes gleam. "I like it."

"Apparently hyenas..." Nicole Vasiliev draws Jessa into a conversation about wildlife, taking attention off us.

"Little elf," I rumble. "You know what you're inviting."

"Do I?" She blinks up at me.

Leaning over, I whisper in her ear. "A spanking."

"I hope so!" she whispers back.

"How are your knickers?" I know the answer full well.

She blushes and smiles and I love that I can still do that to her after all this time.

"The next generation of the London Mafia Syndicate is going to be terrifying," Lev Vasiliev comments, as he also seems to have returned from checking on his kids.

"And a long time in the future," says Dexter Streatham darkly.

"What age were you when you took over Streatham, Dexter?" Angel asks pointedly.

"Fifteen," he admits, with an annoyed downward flick of his eyebrows. "But that's not the point—"

"My girls would be ready at fifteen," says Artem, the Mayfair kingpin.

"Any of our girls would be terrifying at any age." Anderson leans back in his chair and pats his belly. "Great food by the way, thanks King's Cross."

"You're welcome." I squeeze Bella's knee and wink at her. She really does the best job with this party.

"They're too young to be involved with or know about the mafia," Anwyn says. She's the wife of the Westminster kingpin, and they're both a bit posh and serious.

"What, like I was?" Dexter Streatham taps his fork meaningfully on the table.

"Yes, exactly like you were." Sophia Streatham takes her husband's hand and squeezes it.

"Like I've said before." Marco Brent raises his voice over the babble that follows this. This is not the only discussion we've had on this point. "They're going to find out sooner or later. You have to have a strategy for telling them."

"Hmm." I'm not yet convinced.

"I'm still telling ours it's tomato ketchup," says Vito Blackwood with an expressive Italian movement of his hands. He's easy to identify of the three Blackwood triplets, because of the hint of an accent in his voice.

"They don't believe you," counters his brother. Possibly Severino, or maybe Rafe. I can never tell them apart. "You'd never have ketchup in your house when you could have passata."

"Like Father Christmas, the belief is not the point," replies Vito's wife, Cassie.

"Blood doesn't even look like ketchup!" protests Kane Anderson.

"Claim it's paint, that's the right thing," says Jasper Booth, kingpin of Fulham. And he'd know. He has more kids than any of us.

An argument breaks out about what blood looks most like, and what to tell inquiring young minds, until there's a cough and the ting-ting of a spoon.

It takes a couple of attempts to get the rowdier parts of the party to quieten down.

"I want to take this opportunity to propose a toast," Westminster says. At the foot of the table the kingpin of Angel rolls his eyes. "To the spirit of friendship and cooperation that the London Mafia Syndicate was founded upon—"

"You mean the London *Maths* Club," Artem interrupts and Westminster sighs.

"And I thought the point of the Maths Club was to avoid telling Canary Wharf's wife that he wasn't a goodie two shoes CEO?" Nikolai Edmonton calls. "That's hardly the same thing."

"Mobsters And Thugs Hate Singing carols," says Marco Brent.

His wife cracks up. "You say that like you don't love carols!"

There's a hard thump on the table, and everyone turns.

"To our wives, and our children." Fulham says with remarkable calm given how many children he has.

There's an echo from every man at the table, because we can all agree with that. Fulham manages to not immediately make doe eyes at his wife, which to be honest, is more than I achieve. My chin moves of its own accord to look at Bella. She's smiling up at me, and fuck, how did I get this lucky?

So many perfect Christmases with this woman, and so many gifts from her: our kids and special memories.

"And there's a milestone to celebrate," Richmond calls out once our glasses are set down again. "Days since last kidnap is now sixty-seven, a new high!"

"Outstanding. Well done, us," Marco Brent mutters cynically. Lambeth's wife Jessa catches the eye of Brent's wife Felicity and they chink glasses with a giggle.

"I really ought to kidnap you. Make sure you're not left out," I whisper to Bella as there are more laughs about the lack of kidnaps. It seems like half the London Maths Club got their wives by morally dubious means. To be fair, it's not like I'm in the clear on this one. "I watched my innocent virgin camgirl nanny touch herself" is no better than "I abducted the woman I wanted to marry". If there had been any potential for harm to Bella, I'd have seized her in a heartbeat.

"We can do that any evening you like," Bella replies. "Twice on Sunday."

"Alright, alright," Westminster says, and although his words are impatient, his tone is indulgent. Like the murderous mafia bosses he has around him are just errant school boys. "It's time for Secret Santa."

Several people groan, but I grin. Bella organises this as well, and it's the highlight we've all been pretending not to be excited about, like we're the kids, not our offspring at the other table.

"All credit to King's Cross for organising this, and the excellent meal we've all enjoyed." Westminster raises his glass to Bella and me, and I indicate my wife and raise a glass with everyone else.

"The premise, as you know, of Secret Santa—"

"Anonymous presents, yeah, yeah, yeah, we know. Let's do the thing," Artem calls, and there's a ripple of laughter.

Westminster shakes his head, picks up the Santa hat

from somewhere, and goes to the pile of presents. "Okay, first up." He checks the label. "Blackwood."

"Here!" All three triplets say in unison, and Westminster slings the present to where they're sitting.

"Catch." Rafe snatches it out of the air on the way to Vito, who groans.

"Lina," Anwyn says, having donned a Santa hat and joined her husband under the tree. She passes the gifts out in a more conventional way than her husband.

"Why don't we do the Secret Santa gift distribution?" I ask Bella in an undertone.

"Because you told me the first year that if you saw me in a Santa hat in public you'd be forced to make me pay for being a tease all night afterwards," Bella tells me quietly. "And after you made good on that, I believed you."

"Ohhhh." Yes, I remember now. "That does sound fun though."

"It was," she agrees. "But also, the Westminsters like to feel important, and we indulge them since it's Christmas."

Around us coloured paper is being ripped open and there are oohhs and ahhs at the gifts. There is a strict and low budget for the gifts, so things don't get out of hand, as they did the second year we had the party when someone gifted a briefcase of cash to Blackstone. The Scot was not amused.

"Bella." Anwyn places a prettily wrapped book-shaped package next to Bella's plate.

"Ooh thank you!" Bella takes it.

"No, thank you for organising all this."

Bella pulls Anwyn in for a hug and they giggle something about their book club. Bella lets out a high-pitched squeak of excitement when she unwraps her present to reveal a very fancy edition of a book with a skull and moths on the cover. The women have their own more mature and sensible Secret Santa and they mainly give books.

"Sprayed edges! Thank you!" she says to the table at large. "And it's signed, oh my god!"

"Happy Christmas, Lucas." Westminster claps me on the shoulder and offers a long rectangular parcel to me.

"Thanks, Ben." We always call each other by our first names, unlike most of the mafia bosses who are happy to be called their territory name, and that consideration is why we accept him as the leader of the Maths Club. He's smart, and thoughtful. I've never told him that I prefer to be called Lucas, but he figured it out.

"I think it's another train, sorry about that."

I shake my head and sigh, but I'm laughing. "Christmas traditions. My son Frank loves them almost as much as he loves cars, don't worry."

"Ooo, is it a vintage locomotive?" Bella looks up from her book, and Ben slips away.

I shake the parcel and there's the slight rattle of wheels. "Could be a dildo."

Bella snorts.

I'm halfway through tearing it open—I was right, it's a rare collectable train—when there's a bang on the table.

"Who got me this?" Angel holds up an abacus.

There's a roar of laughter as everyone takes it in.

"It's because of that time you didn't stop firing at that guy," Brent says. "You clearly need to learn how to count."

"So it was you?" Angel demands, and Brent holds his hands up and shakes his head.

"It was a genius present," Bella whispers to me.

"Ah!" Angel doesn't miss a thing. Not surprising given his nickname as the dark shadow. "King's Cross! Always on time. I should have known."

I incline my head. "You're not offended are you?"

Angel grins suddenly. "Neit. It's perfect. I've been looking for one for my middle daughter. She struggles with maths."

"You can learn together," I say dryly.

There's a shout of disbelief from the other end of the table.

"A glock? Seriously? I didn't think you guys cared." Edmonton turns it over in his hand experimentally. "It's super light. Is it printed?"

"For fucks sake do not point that at me," snarls Rhys

Cavendish, the kingpin of Canary Wharf, "I thought we said—"

"Yeah, careful." Edmonton's wife leans over and stabs the gun through the barrel with a short knife. "It's really dangerous."

There's a gasp as it breaks apart with a crack.

The outside creases, shiny and silver and inside it's brown.

"Chocolate." Edmonton's Russian accent is more pronounced as he's surprised. "A chocolate gun."

And then everyone around the table is laughing.

Edmonton picks up a piece of chocolate and stuffs it into his mouth, then grinning, pops a section between his wife's lips.

"No, I..." Then the chocolate is in her mouth, and Edmonton has found the wrapped bullets inside the chocolate gun, and is throwing them across the table. Angel catches one, and another lands in Dimitri Voronov's coffee.

"Oh god, stop." Lotte Edmonton has managed to swallow her chocolate, but is laughing so hard her nose is dripping. Edmonton pulls her into his arms and presses her face to his shirt, grinning even as his wife continues to be wracked with giggles.

"That's real love," sighs Bella happily. "Would you let me wipe my nose on your shirt?"

"Well, I've left the house with your girl cum on my

cheeks, so I think the answer is obvious," I reply, tugging a strand of her hair playfully.

"There's no way in hell this was under the spend limit." Canary Wharf waves a solid gold calculator.

"It was," replies Croydon mildly.

"Stealing doesn't count." Canary Wharf arches one eyebrow. "You have to take it back."

"I wouldn't steal!" Anderson replies, affronted.

"Threats?"

"No. I have dignity."

"Bribes."

"What do you take me for?" Anderson pretends to be affronted.

"Brent," says Lambeth wryly.

"Bribes get things done," says Marco Brent matter of factly.

"A morally grey kingpin with a reputation for killing people who get in your way." Canary Wharf replies with a shake of his head.

"Mm." Anderson nods seriously. "Fair. But actually, this *was* a free gift."

"Free." Rafe Blackwood cuts into the conversation, and is clearly sceptical.

"Yep. Totally free." Anderson's smile is almost angelic.

"What did you buy to get that?" I ask, getting what his trick was.

"A car." Anderson doesn't even look embarrassed. He seems pleased with himself. Smug even.

"Did you need a car?" I ask.

He shrugs. "One of the children will need a car eventually."

Canary Wharf snorts with laughter. "Well, thank you. I appreciate my free gift."

It's all so good natured and Christmasy, I'm overcome with uncharacteristic seasonal good cheer.

I push my chair back and pull Bella into my lap and after a squeal of surprise, she snuggles in.

The feeling of her ripe curves against me, the softness of her silk dress and the way she feels beneath my hand, yielding where I'm hard, causes blood to flow to my cock. Ignoring the rest of the Maths Club around us, I gather her hair in my hand and grip it, pulling her head back until she gasps and looks up at me, pupils dilated until there's a rim of dark blue.

"I love you, little elf. I can't wait to get you home." There's a special present I'd like to give my wife this Christmas.

Before I can kiss Bella, there's a tap on my elbow, and I turn to find Sylvie there, escaped from the kid's table, and wearing totally unseasonal bunny ears.

"Daddy, please can I marry Volody?"

THANKS

Thank you for reading, I hope you enjoyed it.

Want to read a little more Happily Ever After? Click to get exclusive epilogues and free stories! or head to EvieRoseAuthor.com

If you have a moment, I'd really appreciate a review wherever you like to talk about books. Reviews, however brief, help readers find stories they'll love.

Love to get the news first? Follow me on your favored social media platform - I love to chat to readers and you get all the latest gossip.

If the newsletter is too much like commitment, I recommend following me on BookBub, where you'll just get new release notifications and deals.

- amazon.com/author/evierose
- bookbub.com/authors/evie-rose
- instagram.com/evieroseauthor
- tiktok.com/@EvieRoseAuthor

INSTALOVE BY EVIE ROSE

Grumpy Bosses

Older Hotter Grumpier

My billionaire boss catches me reading when I should be working. And the punishment...?

Tall, Dark, and Grumpy

When my boss comes to fetch me from a bar, I'm expecting him to go nuts that I'm drunk and described my fake boyfriend just like him. But he demands marriage...

Silver Fox Grump

He was my teacher, and my first off-limits crush. Now he's my stalker, and my boss.

Stalker Kingpins

Spoiled by my Stalker

From the moment we lock eyes, I'm his lucky girl... But there's a price to pay

Kingpin's Baby

I beg the Kingpin for help... And he offers marriage.

Owned by her Enemy

I didn't expect the ruthless new kingpin—an older man, gorgeous and hard—to extract such a price for a ceasefire: an arranged marriage.

His Public Claim

My first time is sold to my brother's best friend

Pregnant by the Mafia Boss

Baby Proposal

My boss walked in on me buying "magic juice" online... And now he's demanding to be my baby's daddy!

Groom Gamble

I accidentally gave my hot boss my list of requirements for a perfect husband: tall, gray eyes, nice smile, big d*ck. High sperm count.

Kingpin's Nanny

My grumpy boss bought my whole evening as a camgirl!

London Mafia Bosses

Captured by the Mafia Boss

I might be an innocent runaway, but I'm at my friend's funeral to avenge her murder by the mafia boss: King.

Taken by the Kingpin

Tall, dark, older and dangerous, I shouldn't want him.

Stolen by the Mafia King

I didn't know he has been watching me all this time.

I had a plan to escape. Everything is going perfectly at my wedding rehearsal dinner until *he* turns up.

Caught by the Kingpin

The kingpin growls a warning that I shouldn't try his patience by attempting to escape.

There's no way I'm staying as his little prisoner.

Claimed by the Mobster

I'm in love with my ex-boyfriend's dad: a dangerous and powerful mafia boss twice my age.

Snatched by the Bratva

I have an excruciating crush on this man who comes into the coffee shop. Every day. He's older, gorgeous, perfectly dressed. He has a Russian accent and silver eyes.

Kidnapped by the Mafia Boss

I locked myself in the bathroom when my date pulled out a knife. Then a tall dark rescuer crashed through the door... and kidnapped me.

Held by the Bratva

"Who hurt you?"

Before I know it, my gorgeous neighbour has scooped me up into his arms and taken me to his penthouse. And he won't let me go.

Seized by the Mafia King

I'm kidnapped from my wedding

Filthy Scottish Kingpins

Forbidden Appeal

He's older and rich, and my teenage crush re-surfaces as I beg the former kingpin to help me escape a mafia arranged marriage. He stares at me like I'm a temptress he wants to banish, but we're snowed in at his Scottish castle.

Captive Desires

I was sent to kill him, but he's captured me, and I'm at his mercy. He says he'll let me go if I beg him to take his...

Eager Housewife

Her best friend's dad is advertising for a free use convenient housewife, and she's the perfect applicant.